C. E. KEEFER

The Mark of Enchantment

Abaddon Series Book 1

First edition

ISBN: 978-0-578-94851-5

Cover art by Natalia Junquerira
Editing by Tim Marquitz

This book was professionally typeset on Reedsy.
Find out more at reedsy.com

This book is dedicated to my loving husband, Gerald Keefer. He supported and helped push me to finish when I thought I never would. It is also dedicated to my good friend, Chelsea Higley, without her this book never would have made it to publishing.

Contents

Prologue

It had been five millennia since Abaddon had seen magic in the lands. No one but the elves knew for sure what banished it, and they would not tell. It came as no surprise when elves entered the human cities and ran rampant. They stole, raped, and murdered innocent humans. Their speed and strength like nothing the humans had seen before. The elves possessed a power long forgotten. There appeared to be no hope for the world of Abaddon.

That was until a man showed up in Roseden, the capital of Ditrem. This man could be no older than forty, yet his hair was white as snow, without a trace of color. A raven sat perched atop his shoulder. If one didn't know any better, they would think it was a statue.

The man's slate-gray eyes softened as he listened to the tales of the inhabitants. They told him of the elves and their recent changes in behavior. Many were surprised he did not know of the dilemma. How could someone not know about the elves who attacked them almost daily?

The man felt moved by their plight and bound to give aid. Stepping out into the square, he raised his right hand. He murmured under his breath and a light glowed from within it. This light grew brighter until it reached a point no one could see anything else. When the light finally dimmed, and the people blinked to readjust their eyes, the elves disappeared from the town. They evaporated, leaving nothing behind. The elves in all the towns and cities in Abaddon disappeared. The plague was over, and people rejoiced at the end of their long nightmare.

The remaining elves in the wilds were charged with the crimes committed and were banished from the mainland. Many elves claimed no part of the massacre and had no idea what caused the small number to turn savage. They were set to live on a small island off the coast of Soeric, named Dwaliwin. However, King Pierce of Soeric felt pity for those unjustly charged. In his eyes, those who did not physically commit the crimes could be innocent.

He granted pardons and safe harbor to those who chose to stay and live within the country's borders. Many left, not wanting to stay where they were hated. Only a small number stayed behind, unwilling to leave the home they had always known.

The attacks on the human cities were over, and order was restored. The man who cast out what was later called the *unspeakable evil* had returned peace to Abaddon. He was known as Syler Acosta.

Chapter 1

Fi Silvera sat on her humble bed, fighting the urge to go back to sleep. The bed had found a perfect level of comfort that begged her to stay longer. It had taken all of her willpower just to sit up, let alone stand. She knew leaving her room meant morning chores on the farm. Cleaning out horse stalls and bringing hay to the cows did not sound inviting to her. On the other hand, if she didn't go, she would have to deal with her uncle and cousin. That sounded even less appealing.

Begrudgingly, she pulled her body off her bed and shambled across her bedroom to her door. A knot in the wood floor caught her toe, and Fi jolted with pain. She picked up her feet as to not catch another one. The bedroom door opened to a small hallway, and the bathroom lay on the other side. She opened the door, finding it unoccupied, and entered, shutting the door behind her.

The bathroom was small and only had a sink with a pitcher of water and a small shelf. The small white pedestal sink offered no source of storage in the room. Not that there was much need. She had no soaps or towels to store since, if she wanted a bath, she would have to go outside. The walls of the bathroom looked like much of the house.

Its cold stone bricks were a deep smoke gray color, making the room appear smaller than it was. A light had been placed on the opposite wall to help illuminate it. With no windows, the light was needed at all times of the day.

She splashed water on her face and hoped it would waken her mind to the chores ahead. Fi caught sight of herself in the simple round mirror hung in front of her. Although she had slept through the night, she felt as though she had been up at least half of it. Her suntanned, heart-shaped face gave way to how tired she felt. Her jade green doe eyes had deep bags under them. They loomed in a dark purple reminiscent of a violet blooming on a warm day. How could she be this tired? She stared at the bags hopelessly, trying to will them away. After a few minutes, she gave a loud sigh, giving up on a hopeless task. Her full pink lips frowned in frustration.

Leaving the bathroom, Fi took four steps across the hall and was back in her room. Before she got ready for the day, she applied a lotion she had used since she was a child. Her uncle Byron told her that her skin was extra sensitive to the sun, even if she wore clothing. There were elves nearby, friends of Byron's, who made a special ointment for her. As long as she put it on in the mornings, the sun could no longer damage her skin.

She dug through her old cedar trunk at the end of the bed, hoping to find something clean. As full as it was, not much of it would be wearable. She had a bad habit of waiting to wash clothes until she had nothing left to wear. It was a habit she told herself countless times she would work but never did. She finally found a pair of cotton brown pants, which hugged her around her hips, and a plain white blouse that lay loosely across her slender body. She knew white was a bad idea working on a farm but threw it on anyway due to lack of choices.

She came down the stairs to the smell of food being cooked. Her cousin Mariah was in the kitchen cooking bacon. The smell wafted through the entire first floor, making Fi's stomach growl loudly.

Fi and Mariah were the same height, around five-six, but were built very differently. Mariah was a thick young woman in her mid-twenties, three years older than Fi. You could see the years of manual labor on her body. Fi, on the other hand, was lean, and her body hid much of her muscle. Mariah's shoulder-length mud-brown hair was a stark contrast to Fi's platinum blonde locks pulled back into a tight braid to her waist.

It was hard to believe sometimes they were related. The only thing about Mariah Fi truly envied was that Mariah had the chest of a woman. Fi's breasts reminded her of a girl just going through the changes, and then her body just stopped like a cruel joke.

The kitchen had freshly baked bread on the counter next to a large bowl of fruits. The pan Mariah used had six large strips of bacon that looked ready to be taken out. Fi knew if she hurried, she would be able to fry herself up an egg or two when Mariah was done with the pan. Eggs always tasted better when cooked in the leftover bacon grease.

"Oversleep again this morning?" Mariah shot over her shoulder. "I can understand why someone like you would need more beauty sleep."

Glaring, Fi retorted, "I didn't even oversleep that much. You act as though it is hours past sunrise." Fi went to grab a plate of food as her stomach growled yet again. She tried to move past Mariah in the small kitchen.

"The sun has been up for three hours already," Mariah shot back. "You were supposed to start your chores two hours ago."

Fi stopped in her tracks and looked at Mariah. *There is no way it is that late,* she thought. How could she have not seen the sun out her window this morning? Was she so caught up in her thoughts she didn't even look for the obvious, like what time it was?

"You have got to be kidding me. Shit!" Fi yelled as she ran out the door towards the barns to muck the manure from the horse stalls. She couldn't believe she had overslept that much and not realized. How was she still so tired after getting extra sleep?

Outside, she saw it was indeed well past sunrise. The sun had begun its ascent into the sky, providing the farm with plenty of light. While they did not have a large farm in comparison to their neighbors, it still took Mariah, Uncle Byron, and herself all day to tend to it.

The cow pasture was on her left as it extended out towards the surrounding forest, but never too close to attract the attention of a roaming Fiend. The horse barn and chicken coop were on the right side of the farm. Fi walked the all too familiar trail to the horses when an image flashed in her mind.

A large stone castle tucked away into a remote mountainous country. The trees looked diseased the closer they grew to the castle. As if the soil itself plagued them. They grew, craning their trunks away from the castle. What kind of place has nature itself trying to escape it?

An older man stood inside, talking with others. His white hair cut close to his head made him look as though he was in the military at some point. A well-cared for beard lay across his face, almost framing it. He was in a deep discussion with others around him.

She couldn't make out who they were or much of what they looked like. Their dark armor hid the details. The man's slate-gray eyes showed anger unlike anything Fi had seen before. He turned and looked straight at her. She couldn't help but shake when his eyes met hers. Darkness emanated off his being. She tried to back up, but her feet appeared rooted to the ground.

As suddenly as it appeared, Fi's vision cleared, and her Uncle Byron was shaking her, yelling her name.

"Fi! Fi, can you hear me?" Byron yelled. His large muscular body sweated from the fear of her being unresponsive.

Byron Summerheld was a man unlike any other. He had worked like a mule his whole life to make his farm the way it was after his father passed. He was the kind of man who would do anything for their farm and neighbors. Byron was the one everyone called when they needed help or advice. It took a lot to ruffle him. But now, his azure blue eyes stared, watching for any sort of response he could get from her.

"Huh?" was all she could mutter. Fi's eyebrows pulled together, not understanding what just happened. She trembled in his hands as she recalled what she had just seen. She decided not to tell him since she was most likely recalling a bad dream from the previous night.

"What is going on?" Byron asked. "One minute, I am ready to give you a good lashing for oversleeping, and the next, you are standing in the middle of the farm, not moving. You stopped as if your feet no longer knew how to move." His hands were firmly pressed against her shoulders, as though she would slip away from him at any moment.

"It was nothing really," she tried to lie. Her stomach sunk when she discovered her feet truly would not move during that weird moment. "Must still be half-asleep. I ran here straight out of bed since I was running behind. I should probably get to the chores before it gets even later," she blurted out her response a lot faster than she meant.

It didn't help her in trying to convince Uncle Byron she didn't have some weird, crazy episode. She waited to see if her uncle bought her half-concocted story. He didn't appear to but didn't press her about it anymore. He simply released her shoulders and took a step back.

She moved past him quickly to start her chores. Uncle Byron watched her head down the hill towards the horse barn. He knew things would change faster than he hoped they would. Truthfully, he hoped these days would never come at all.

Once he was out of sight, Fi slowed her stride. She tried to make sense of what she had seen in her mind. She took a deep breath. When not near the barns, the air was crisp and refreshing. It had a subtle scent of pine from the forest that was pleasant. It always had a way of calming her and bringing her brain back to focus. The forest made her wonder what more was outside the family farm.

The sun had risen enough to beat down on her, warming her cold sweat. She hoped the day wouldn't be too hot since many of the chores involved manual labor and was torture if the sun was unforgiving.

She decided to start with the horse stalls. It was the least taxing physically, and when she finished, she could work outside in the fresh air she longed for. She walked toward the old brown barn that had seen better days. The pine wood planks holding it together were regularly replaced due to rot and mold. Even now, a few boards bowed from the recent rains. She hoped they would dry out and not need to be replaced. It was never an easy task replacing boards on the top half of the barn.

Fi opened one of the two barn doors and slipped in. She was struck by the smell of the horses. There was the obvious scent of manure that tended to overpower every other smell. However, the barn had undertones of fresh hay and pine wood. This barn was one of Fi's favorite places, besides the wonderful open feeling of the field. Whenever Fi felt overwhelmed or needed to get away, she would come to the barn and be with the horses. Many times, Fi felt more comfortable around them than people.

The barn had six horse stalls surrounding a spacious area in the middle. Above the open area of the barn lay a hay loft filled with fresh hay for the horses. Fi often thought it was teasing the horses having the hay so they could see it and not get to it. Uncle Byron always told her she was being overly sensitive, and they were just horses.

There were eight beams spaced out, holding both the barn and the loft up. An area to the right of the entrance held the accessories for the horses. This included their blankets, bridles, saddles, curry combs, and tools for their hooves.

Her favorite horse, Hero, was in his stall in the far back, chewing on some hay Uncle Byron placed that morning. Fi walked over to muck his stall first. Hero was a palomino quarter horse. His body resembled a deep caramel, with a cream-colored mane and tail. He was taller than most of the other horses. Many of Uncle Byron's other horses were plain bays, so Hero had always stood out.

"Morning, Hero," she called out so he knew she was there. He perked his ears up and shifted them in her direction. "You need to move so I can clean." She opened his stall door, sliding in.

Hero just stood there, staring at her. His amber brown eyes offered a look of *make me move.* He was always a stubborn horse and liked to play as though he had no idea what he was expected to do. Mariah refused to work with him since he made her nervous. His demeanor never made Fi apprehensive. Most times, he was all bark and no bite. Fi stepped into the stall and gave him a nudge. Hero nudged her back in response.

"Hero, move your big butt out of the way so I can clean. I swear, you are so stubborn one could mistake you for being a mule." Fi tried to shove him over so she could get past. Hero thrust his hip into her, knocking her down. Unfortunately, since it had yet to have cleaned, her once white shirt now covered in horse manure. It looked like a brown shirt rather than white. She knew wearing it was a bad idea.

"Seriously, Hero. Again?" Fi exclaimed.

This was not their first *dispute*. Hero almost seemed to laugh as he whinnied at her. Fi picked up a small amount of manure in her hand and threw it at Hero's upper shoulder. She had an uncanny ability to hit a target she aimed for. Hero continued to whinny as he moved to allow her further in the stall, but she went over to the metal water pump and cleaned off her hands first. It took her about fifteen minutes to get Hero's stall all cleaned out. Once she finished, she brought in a silver bucket and cleaned the manure from Hero's shoulder.

Fi had no problems with the rest of the stalls. She always had a way with animals. Not that she could talk to them, but there was almost always an understanding. They knew where she needed them to move and would go there. Well, all but Hero, anyway. It made doing her chores much easier than if Mariah tried to do them.

An hour later, the barn was fully mucked, and Fi stepped outside. She opened the barn doors leading to the horse field. Then she led each horse out so they could graze. Many of them took off, happily enjoying the feeling of the grass and sun. Molly, who was Uncle Byron's horse, was older than the others and simply walked out into the field. She was a pretty basic bay with stockings on all four of her feet.

As Hero was led out, he nuzzled Fi. He might be a pain sometimes, but he really was a sweet horse. While he listened well to Uncle Byron, he had taken a liking to Fi. They stood just outside the large barn doors, watching the other horses as they calmed. With one last nuzzle, Hero made his way to the rest of the herd.

After finishing in the barn, Fi moved to the cow pasture to put out bales of hay. With summer ending in a couple of months, they had to start feeding the cows hay to prepare them for winter. It was a ten-minute walk from the barn to reach the hay pile, and Fi took her time. She may have been behind on her chores, but she wanted to enjoy the feeling of openness as much as she could. It was hard to be in the same place doing the same thing every day. She tried not to be too upset by it because many had less than they did. She just couldn't help her restless heart.

Once she reached the hay bales, Fi bent down and picked one up. Uncle Byron liked to pack the hay tight so it required fewer trips to feed all the cows. Each bale weighed close to fifty pounds. Fi was a slender twenty-one-year-old. It did not look as though she should be able to move the bales by herself so easily, but Fi had much more muscle than it appeared. She was able to put them out to the cows with minimal effort. She tossed them over the fence before climbing over.

The cows were out in the field, currently grazing on the grass. There were presently fifteen cows. It was a smaller number than they normally had at one time. They tried to breed the females earlier that spring but, unfortunately, none of them fell pregnant. Fi was thankful their bull, Tidus, was housed in a separate pasture. He had a real mean streak, so Uncle Byron was the only one who ever dealt with him.

Once over the fence, Fi broke down the bales so the cows would have an easier time getting the hay out. By this time, the cows had noticed her and made their way over to her. A few of the younger cows kept their distance, unsure if they could trust her. The older cows showed no fear and came within a few feet to eat the hay. The position of the sun informed Fi it was almost noon.

The sun had decided it was going to burn hot in the sky. Fi wiped the sweat from her brow and was thankful for the small breeze coming across the field. It was times like this that Fi was jealous of Mariah's shorter hair. She picked the braid off her neck to try and cool down. Fi's stomach grumbled. reminding her she ran out before eating breakfast that morning. She decided to head back to the house to eat and cool off.

Fi began the long, hot walk back to the house. She moved at a faster pace than she had that morning. It didn't take long before the farmhouse was on the horizon. The stone was uneven but still sturdy. There were once beautiful wood beams over the doors, but time and wear had left them worn and decayed. Coming from the fields, she could see her bedroom window. It had the best view in the evening when the sun set.

As she reached the house and went inside, Uncle Byron eyed her from the kitchen table. His blue eyes searched for any signs she was not acting like herself. He finished at the table and went to place his plate in the sink. Mariah wiped down the dark wood counters and stored any uneaten food.

He had to scoot around her since the kitchen was small and could barely accommodate two people. It was a narrow walkway with a stove and storage cabinets on one side and a counter on the other. There was some storage below the counter they used for cooking utensils.

"What is that smell?" Mariah exclaimed as Fi came into the kitchen. She crinkled her nose, causing her freckles to move together into a singular tan spot. Fi forgot Hero knocked her down earlier. She must have gotten used to the smell throughout the day.

"That would be me. Hero and I had a small disagreement again," Fi replied as she went to get food. Now that she could smell the food, her stomach would not stop reminding her to eat.

"No, you don't," Mariah said, standing in Fi's way. Fi stopped suddenly. "You clean yourself up before you go anywhere near the rest of the house. You stink to high heaven."

With a loud sigh, Fi turned around and went back outside to pump water from the well. Her stomach protested her abandoning the food.

The tub was to the north side of the house. It was a simple brown clay basin that sat elevated on blocks to accommodate a small fire patch underneath. She started the fire under the tub and filled it with water. Once it was full enough, she undressed and climbed in. The water was just warm enough it wasn't freezing. The cool water was welcoming to her hot skin. The only benefit of a hot bath would have been to soothe her muscles from the hard work of the morning. She grabbed the lye soap and cleaned herself.

Once she was finished, she crawled out and washed her clothes. She hung them to dry on the clothesline and ran inside to grab a new set. Fi hoped no one was in the kitchen since she had no way to cover herself. Being kicked out of the house did not give her a chance to grab a towel from her room. She felt relieved when she peeked her head through the back door, and no one was in sight. Fi assumed they went back out to finish their afternoon chores.

She walked past the living room and went up the stairs. Mariah's room was the first room at the top, and Uncle Byron's was the next door. She passed the bathroom on the left and finally came to her room across from it.

It was the smallest bedroom in the house, tidy but comfortable. The stone walls mimicked those in the rest of the house, and the floors were dark brown wood. Fi wasn't sure what kind of wood they were made of, but the color went well with the stone. Her bed frame was made of pine and was just big enough for her to sleep comfortably on. A matching nightstand sat next to it, holding a kerosene lamp. Besides her trunk, there was a large oak armoire. While most people kept clothes in them, she mainly kept her towels, a bow for hunting, a few books, and extra blankets.

Fi came to live with her Uncle Byron when she was just a baby. Her mother had her out of wedlock and could not bear to look at her, let alone raise her. Fi was proof of her transgressions and shame. To this day, Fi had never met her mother and knew absolutely nothing of her father. The only knowledge she had was his last name. The name her mother decided to give her, Silvera.

Thankfully, Uncle Byron had a soft heart and took her in. He always treated her as if she were his own. At times, it felt as though Mariah was jealous of how close she and Uncle Byron had become, but she would, too, if her father grew a bond with someone other than herself.

It was not as if Mariah and Uncle Byron did not get along or have anything in common. On the contrary, the problem was they were so similar they tended to butt heads regularly. They both had ideas on how the farm should be run and, many times, they varied greatly. It caused them to argue constantly. Mariah lost more often than she won, which caused a small sense of resentment.

Fi grabbed a white towel out of her armoire and dried herself off. Sufficiently dry, Fi dug through the large trunk again, looking for something to wear. She thought she really needed to get better about cleaning and organizing her clothing. She settled on another pair of brown cotton pants, which were a little big for her but had a tie on the top so she could cinch them. She was also able to find a light-yellow peasant top that only had a slight smell to it. She then went back to the kitchen to get some well-deserved food.

She ate cold bacon Mariah left out for her, a few biscuits, and some fruit lying on the counter. She sat at the small table just off the kitchen in solitude as Uncle Byron and Mariah were back outside tending to the farm. It seemed like the work was never done. The day started with working, and you worked until a few hours before you went to bed. Nothing ever changed, and the days tended to grow together. The only thing that changed was the type of work required as the seasons changed.

Fi let her mind wander. She often wondered what else was out there in the world. While she was thankful for Uncle Byron's kindness and willingness to take her on, she felt she was meant for more. She longed to see other cities and countries. What was it like in Moildan, the country of gold? She had heard stories that buildings we inlaid with gold and shone like jewelry in the sunlight. Or the country of Ditrem, who had a lone Queen. Fi longed to see how other people lived their lives and find her path in life.

Unfortunately, whenever this was mentioned, it was met with strong resistance. There were fiends in the wilderness that would attack travelers when their paths crossed. She was told of horror stories and how the world was still in a state of unrest, wizards born into the world in small numbers. It was unsafe to just go wandering.

Fi knew wizards existed, but they were never supposed to be outside Highbarrow. When a wizard was born, they have a birthmark called The Mark of Enchantment somewhere on their body. That child was watched, and when they are old enough to be weaned from their mother, they are then taken to Highbarrow for training by the great Syler. He was the oldest wizard alive and had saved them many times in the past. It was the only way to keep the wild magic from hurting those by accident.

Unfortunately, the training to tame their magic came at a cost. Families tended to treat sending their child away as a mark of death. Many young wizards wouldn't survive the trials it took to gain control. Even though they were born with magic, their bodies couldn't handle the power, and they died. She didn't know what the mark looked like herself but, obviously, did not have it.

When she finished eating, she washed her plate and returned outside to work on the afternoon chores. The sun was still at its peak and met her with its beaming heat. She cursed the sky for not providing a single cloud as coverage to give her a sense of relief. What an unforgiving sky to torture everyone with its fever.

Picking up the pace, she walked toward the chicken coop to check for any eggs laid since they were collected this morning. The coop was decent-sized and housed about three dozen chickens. The coop itself had seen better days, but it served its purpose and kept the chickens safe. The chickens needed to be checked morning, afternoon, and night.

The coop was warm and muggy. While the wired-up windows allowed for a decent breeze, it still could become balmy. The heat never bothered the chickens much. They had a small door out the back, which led to an enclosed outside pen if they ever wanted to stretch their legs.

The chickens seemed annoyed at the disturbance, and a few pecked at her hand. Fi hated the chickens, and doing anything with them was her least favorite part of the farm. They were the one animal that didn't seem to have a connection with her. If they did, they didn't seem to care.

After collecting the eggs, Fi headed back to the house and placed the eggs on the counter to be washed and stored. Depending on how many Mariah collected this morning, they should have plenty to bring to the festival tomorrow. It was rare their chickens did not provide enough eggs to give them a surplus. They were livestock that almost always brought them a profit for the farm.

Chapter 2

Feeling drained from the chores and heat, Fi decided to forgo more work and headed back to the barn to relax with Hero. Her right shoulder felt sore from the day's chores, so a rest sounded great. She grabbed an apple off the counter to bring him as a treat. No hard feelings about being knocked down earlier that morning. She walked out the back door and went straight to the barn, the sun now thankfully hidden behind clouds. The sky must have felt her disdain and offered cover.

As she approached the barn, she took a final breath of fresh air. She felt the stress melt away from her. Fi snuck into the barn before anyone could see her. The horses were still out in the pasture, so she walked past the empty stalls to the door that led outside. Trigger and Brandy were at the far end of the field, grazing. They were easy to tell apart since Trigger was about a hand taller than Brandy. Cinnamon snoozed under the shade of a tree, her white patch on her nose making her stand out in the shadow. Molly and Boots were at the trough guzzling down water.

Hero stood in the shade of the barn, separated from the herd. He never fully integrated with the other horses. There was never any fighting between them, but Hero kept his distance when he could. His trust issues ran deep from his abuse. Fi walked over to him and offered him the bright red apple. He happily ate it and rested his head on her shoulder.

"Hero, one of these days, you and I will leave this farm. You can run, and I can finally have a life I feel is worth living," she told him.

She felt somewhat guilty for disliking her life, but she couldn't help that she wanted more. She stayed in the pasture with Hero for a half-hour before heading back to the house to finish her chores. It would not be long before Mariah and Uncle Byron came looking for her. If she were caught lounging while everyone was working, she would never hear the end of it, especially after sleeping in that morning.

Fi walked back to the house, set on washing her clothes so she would have clean clothes to wear. Tomorrow, she would need them for sure. She was in her head, trying to think of ways to become more organized and be less of a mess. Time flew by, lost in thought, and she could see the house. Once it was in full view, she saw Uncle Byron talking to someone outside. They appeared to be in a friendly discussion as she approached. As she got closer, she realized it was Erlan Evervine, an elf who came to visit them. Her heart pounded.

She could not explain it, but every time she saw him, she got excited. Her heart always leaped from her chest, and she could not help but smile. Thankfully, he never noticed her strange behavior. Maybe as an elf, he considered it a normal human trait. It worked to her advantage she had acted the same way since she was eight or nine years old.

He turned to look at her. His piercing blue eyes met hers, and he cracked a smile, showing perfect teeth. She ran into his arms, and he swung her around as he had done when she was a child. His long, chestnut brown hair fell across his porcelain face when they stopped.

"What are you doing here?" she asked him, smiling. Erlan always stopped by when he was in town and would often stay with them. He came to trade between Baydell and the nearby elven village of Pirn.

"Oh, you know, business like always. I was hoping to convince your uncle to let me stay here again," Erlan explained. Fi knew asking for permission was an act of respect rather than an allowance.

"Why do you ask every time? You know the answer is always yes," Byron said back to him, chuckling. "Though, since you asked, I say you can only stay if you help at the festival tomorrow. Payment and such." Both men laughed together as old friends do over a dumb joke. When the laughter settled, Erlan leaned into Uncle Byron's ear and spoke softly.

"Byron, I must speak with you. The real reason I have come is the elders have said the time for the prophecy is now. Events are happening, and preparations need to be made," Erlan said quietly. Uncle Byron tensed at the words. Erlan was shorter than Uncle Byron by a good two inches, Byron standing six feet, but he looked smaller in comparison in that moment.

"Fi, go inside while we talk," he said through gritted teeth. Fi went to argue, but he shot her a look that told her now was not the time. She wanted to go back and eavesdrop, but she knew if she were caught, she would be in big trouble. The closer she got to the house, the more her right shoulder blade burned. It had been sore most of the day, but this pain was worse and more concentrated. It almost felt like she had been hit by something hot, or she had been bitten. She had never felt anything this painful in her entire life. She forced herself into the back door of the house.

As she entered the house, she collapsed in the doorway, barely crossing the threshold. The burning grew more intense, as if someone branded her skin with a hot iron. It took everything she had not to pass out. Mariah came running outside, yelling for Uncle Byron. It did not take long for the pain to hit its peak and remain intense. Fi's breath caught as sweat dripped off her face. She fell to the floor, no longer having the strength to stay up. All her energy was being used just to breathe.

"What's going on?" Byron exclaimed as he ran to the house. His stomach hit the floor when he saw Fi on the ground, and his breath caught in his throat. There was scarlet blood on her right shoulder blade, soaking through her shirt. The blood ran down her arm and created crimson pools onto the floor beneath her. He quickly scooped her up and brought her upstairs to her bedroom. Fi breathed heavily and felt herself slipping in and out of consciousness.

"What's wrong with her?" Mariah demanded, standing in Fi's doorway. In the confusion and chaos, Byron did not realize she stood there. During those moments, he had forgotten completely about Mariah. His attention was focused on Fi, and Mariah did not need to see what was happening.

"Nothing to concern yourself with. Either finish your chores or stay in your room until I tell you to come out. We need to focus on Fi, and you would just get in the way," Uncle Byron snapped. He needed her away from the scene. She took a step back in surprise. He had never spoken that way to her before. She went back down the stairs and began cleaning the blood off the floor.

Erlan was close behind Byron, whispering in elvish under

his breath. Fi wished she knew what they were saying, but she did not understand Elvish other than basic pleasantries. There was no humor in whatever Erlan said. Uncle Byron's face grew tenser the more they conversed. His face appeared to have aged from the last time she saw him outside. She worried something was terribly wrong. Was she dying?

Uncle Byron laid her down on the bed, with her back facing up. The sheets seemed less inviting than they did this morning when she awoke. Their crisp white color slowly being stained, looking like flowers blooming every time a drop touched it.

"I'm going to have to rip your shirt a bit to get a better look at the wound," Byron explained. Fi had a passing thought of one less shirt to wash. "Please, try to hold still. I don't know how bad it is yet."

She nodded and felt her shirt rip enough to expose her shoulders and mid-back. Erlan and Uncle Byron started talking quickly amongst each other and began arguing. Fi could not make out what they said as she missed half of the conversation as she faded in and out of consciousness. Whatever they were arguing about, it seemed as though Uncle Byron won. This did not surprise Fi. Erlan moved next to her on the bed and bent closer.

"I'm going to put a healing salve on your shoulder. It is going to feel cold and sting, but I need you to stay still," Erlan told her softly in her ear. "I will try to be as quick and gentle as I can."

Fi felt his delicate hands touch her bare back, and she uncontrollably shuddered. Once her body was still again, he placed the salve on her back. It felt frigid, as if someone put snow on her instead of medicine. It soothed the burning sensation that had exploded on her shoulder. She breathed in a normal rhythm.

"I am going to need you to lie here awhile while it sets in," he told her. "If you like, I can sit here with you, so you are not alone." Fi went to speak but found she did not have the energy to do so. She nodded, thankful she would not be alone, left to get caught up in her contemplations. In times of crisis, which could be more damaging than the actual problem. Uncle Byron shifted over by the door.

"I will go and talked to Mariah. In all the commotion, I took my frustration out on her," Byron said as he turned to leave, shooting Erlan a look only a father could give before departing the room. Byron may not be Fi's biological father, but he always protected her like she was his own.

Fi was excited to be alone with Erlan. It was rare the two of them were ever alone. Uncle Byron and Mariah were always around. Not that it was intentional, the house just was not very big. She could barely move in her room without anyone noticing. Now, here she was, alone with him, with her back exposed. She blushed, remembering how she currently looked to him.

She had never been with a man. Lying with a man before marriage was a transgression against the temple. Fi did not want to create a child out of wedlock like herself. Though the city they lived in was kind, she would still get looks from the older generation since she did not have a mother and a father. She had liked a few boys in the past, but none worth courting with. Her heart was not set on settling down and being a mother. She wanted more than that life, she wanted adventure.

They sat there in silence for twenty minutes. The minutes were becoming more painful the longer it went on. As much as she wanted someone to be with her, she hated that she sat in silence. It did not help that much of her back was naked to him. She wanted to be distracted by her thoughts, not caused to have more. She wondered about Erlan. Was there some elven woman waiting for him to come home after a trip to the humans? If there was, he never talked about her.

"How are you feeling, Fi?" Erlan asked her after a while. The break-in silence startled her. He seemed perfectly at ease sitting next to her on the bed. She was not sure he had even moved once in the minutes that passed. The burning had completely stopped now, and she felt much better.

"Whatever it was that you put on there made a big difference. I don't even feel pain anymore," Fi explained. "How did you know what to put on there to make it feel better?" She tried to sit up, but her ripped shirt slid down, exposing her chest. It took her a second to react to Erlan being able to see her petite breasts. She quickly grabbed her shirt and pulled it over herself. Fi blushed. She wanted to die in that instant. Erlan calmly sat up from the bed and headed towards the door as if nothing happened.

"I am an elf with many years of medicinal training," he said, turning back to look at her. "I will leave you to put on a new shirt while I explain to Byron you are recovering nicely." With a reassuring smile, he pivoted and walked out of the room.

Fi wanted to just melt into her bed and disappear. How was she supposed to look Erlan in the eye after something like that? She should not even have the feelings she had for him. Relationships between elves and humans were forbidden after the *unspeakable evil* happened. But she could not help how she felt about him. She could not stop her heart from racing when she saw his face. She knew she could never have him, but it did not stop her from wishing.

After a few minutes, she collected herself. Walking over to her trunk, she went digging once again for a shirt. She found an old deep green sleeveless shirt shoved into the bottom corner. It was wrinkled and worn, but it was clean. As she put it on, she felt her shoulder blade. It was as smooth as it was that morning, no brand or trace of a burn.

The shirt hung low in the front, exposing more of her chest than she was remotely comfortable with, especially after what had just happened. She tried to find another shirt but quickly gave up, reminding herself she needed to get better at doing laundry.

An hour passed before Fi decided she had stayed upstairs long enough and headed to the living room. Everyone sat around talking as she came down. Erlan was in an olive-green upholstered chair by the fireplace, its large arms the perfect level for resting your elbows to read a book. Uncle Byron and Mariah sat on the patched-up muddy brown couch adjacent. The couch had been in the house since Fi could remember, and whenever it gained a new hole, Mariah placed a new patch on it. The patches were made from many scraps of fabric, so it had become a couch of many colors.

The fireplace did not need to be lit since late spring and summer nights were almost as warm as the day. Tonight, in particular, was muggy and full of humidity. The house had no way of keeping the heat out so, some nights, it was hard to sleep. After sweating upstairs, Fi needed a large glass of water.

Coming down the stairs, Fi heard conversations between the three of them. They spoke so low it was hard to make out what they were saying. Mariah still sounded upset with Uncle Byron, and it was mainly those two doing the talking. As she emerged at the bottom of the stairs, all conversation stopped. Usually, that was a sign the conversation had been about Fi.

Without glancing into the living room, Fi turned into the kitchen. Her throat felt parched and scratchy. She opened the cupboard and grabbed a small tan clay cup. Using the small hand pump, she filled it with water and drank it down in three gulps. She filled it again and walked into the living room. Fi looked over by the door and saw there was no trace of blood left on the wood.

"Feeling any better?" Erlan asked in a smooth voice. Fi felt herself instantly blush. Thankfully, no one noticed.

"Much better thanks to whatever it was you put on my back," she replied, quickly walking over to sit on the open spot on the couch. "What are we all talking about?" Not wanting to relive what happened, Fi hoped they could pretend it did not happen for now.

"Are you sure, you gave us quite a scare there?" Byron probed. "Are you sure everything feels normal?" Fi felt her back again to be sure it was as it was upstairs. He watched her carefully, leaning towards her.

"Yes, I feel fine. Almost as if it never happened," Fi confirmed. Uncle Byron sunk into the couch. He worried so much for her, which gave Fi guilt about thinking about leaving earlier that day.

"We will have to keep an eye on your shoulder. I do not know what happened, but I am glad Erlan was here to help you. Tonight, we need to talk about the upcoming festival celebrating our new King Elric and his new engagement to Princess Victoria from across the Pisogh Sea to the south." Byron said, "It begins tomorrow, and we have agreed to supply the beef and eggs for the festival. I know we have been working extra hours in order to have everything prepared. Tomorrow, we will need to get to the town market early to get set up. Fi, are you sure you feel well enough to help?"

"As I said, I am fine. I will be up tomorrow to help just as planned," Fi answered. She truly did feel fine. There was no reason something strange like that should stop her if Uncle Byron said Erlan fixed it. Fi looked up at Erlan, who seemed confident what he had done worked.

"We should all get some rest now. Morning will come faster than we think," Byron said. He looked around at everyone, ensuring they understood. "In the morning, we must finish packing the food and loading it into the old wagon. We will need everyone to work hard tomorrow."

"Better have someone willing to go in and wake the sleepy princess over here since she can't even get up for her regular chores, let alone for a festival," Mariah added, gesturing to Fi.

"Really? I hardly ever oversleep, and I still got all the chores done on time. What is your issue, Mariah?" Fi sniped back. While Mariah would poke fun at Fi, her words held a more sinister tone.

"You may have gotten your chores done, but you took your sweet time doing it. I saw you being lazy in the horse pasture while the rest of us were working. You are babied so much around here it is sickening." Mariah said angrily. Something inside Fi snapped, and she could not control her anger.

"What the hell is your problem? I took a half-hour of my day with Hero to recharge. I did not realize that was a crime. I didn't get breakfast and ate a late lunch to ensure I got everything done. I am sorry we cannot all be like you. I want more than just farming, which is all you are ever going to be good for." Fi regretted her words the minute they left her mouth.

She opened her mouth to apologize, but Mariah had stood up from the couch. Her face looked a mix of anger and trying not to cry. With a few quick strides, Mariah had made her way out of the living room and through the kitchen. The back door slammed behind her as she stormed out of the house.

"You have a good heart, Fi, but sometimes you know just what to say to cut the deepest," Byron said, scolding his eyes narrow. "I am going to go talk to her. She may need to cool off, but she cannot be outside by herself. Fiends were spotted at the Porter's farm a few miles down the road." He got up and went outside, looking for Mariah. Fiends would tend to come out after sunset. The armies in Soeric were good about keeping many of the Fiends in small numbers, but there were always the few able to find their way into outlying farms.

Fi and Erlan were left alone yet again. She became conscious of her low shirt and moved slightly away from him. Her breasts were not something men would write home about, but they have been more than slightly exposed today. He must have noticed because he gave her a confused look.

"Are you sure you are okay?" Erlan asked her kindly, "You seem to be acting a little different. Are you sure you don't need me to check you for any more illnesses?" He shifted from the chair and moved onto the couch next to her.

"What? Uh no I'm fine, really just not a fan of this shirt is all, but I have little choices today," she said, thinking how stupid she sounded. She needed to stop being so ridiculous and just see him as he was an elf not human. An elf with a perfectly made a face that looked both hard and soft. Its oval shape allowing his hair to fall perfectly to frame it. An elf with eyes that were a perfect almond shape, creating a look of caring, even if he was not trying. His slender build showed every muscle he had. She shook her head when she realized she was blushing.

"Your face is red. Do you have a fever?" he asked, seeming oblivious she was fine and just embarrassed. He leaned towards her, his long hair falling into his face. "If you need, I can check for you. I am sure I have some herbs that can help with that." *Do elves not blush when embarrassed?*

"No, no really, I am fine," she stuttered out, trying to regain control of herself. Erlan was inches from her face, looking concerned. Just then, Uncle Byron and Mariah came back into the house. The timing could not have been more perfect. Fi had caught herself leaning in to attempt to kiss him. What a mistake that would have been. A wonderful mistake.

"Well, I think I am going to bed! I'll see you guys tomorrow morning," she said quickly as she jumped up and headed towards her room. Erlan's expression turned baffled. Apparently, he did not realize the precarious position they had been in. Uncle Byron looked to Fi, to Erlan, and back to Fi to figure out what he had just interrupted. Fi just smiled weakly and bolted upstairs.

When she opened her bedroom door, she caught sight of the bloodstain on her sheets. A cruel and ugly reminder of what had happened earlier that night. Again, she touched her shoulder blade, feeling nothing but smooth skin. She walked over and changed the sheets on the bed before climbing in. The bed welcomed her after a long and stressful day. She was exhausted after everything today and was hoping this sleep would be more restful than the night before.

Chapter 3

When Fi awoke the next morning, she felt fully rested from an uneventful night's sleep. She must have slept hard since she'd woken in the same position she fell asleep in. Her left arm and leg were stiff. The smell of the fresh sheets begged her to roll over and stay. They still had the scent of drying on the line, lending them a breath of fresh air.

As much as Fi wanted to give into them, she knew she had to get up and get ready for the festival. She sat up, her mattress creaking. Her body protested her movement and ached as she stretched. She reached her hand back under her shirt to feel her shoulder blade again. As it was yesterday, it was as smooth and untouched as it had always been.

Finally standing, Fi walked over to her trunk to grab a fresh set of clothes. Panic set in when a thought came to her. In all the chaos yesterday, she never got any of her clothes cleaned. What was she going to wear to the festival today? Everything she currently owned had the look or smell of the farm on it. She picked up a few shirts to see if any were clear of odor. She crinkled her nose at each one and felt defeated. Then there was a sudden, quiet knock on the door.

"Fi?" Byron said quietly. "Are you awake?" His voice had

a gravel tone to it, which made it sound as though sleep still clung to him. *I am not the last one up today,* she thought.

"Yes, I am. Hold on a second," she responded. Fi slammed the trunk closed and opened her door. Uncle Byron looked as if he had rolled out of bed. His shaggy brown hair was disheveled, and he was still in his white night clothes.

"I forgot to give this to you yesterday," he said as he handed her a light blue dress. "It is a special event, so I dug into my savings and bought you and Mariah something nice to wear." Relief passed over Fi. While she wasn't a big fan of dresses, it gave her something clean to wear.

"It's beautiful, thank you," she responded. It was little things like that Uncle Byron did that made her forget about wanting to leave. He loved her so much and had always wanted what was best for her. He didn't have to buy her nice things when he bought them for Mariah, but he always did. Fi was always included in every family event and was never made to feel like an outsider.

"I will leave you to get dressed," Byron said after Fi took the dress. "I need to get ready and see everything is ready to take to town." He turned and walked back down the hallway to his room.

Fi laid the dress on her bed, looking it over. The blue reminded her of ice, and the reflection it gave when the sun hit it just right. While the dress scooped down in the front, it still led to a sense of modesty. The back of the dress, however, did not come so low. If her hair was up, you would barely see the backs of her shoulders.

As she inspected the sleeves, she saw a small loop at the end. She knew from seeing other women in town this was meant to go around the middle finger. There was a thin matching string belt around the waist of the dress that led the eye to the A-line skirt.

Fi could not imagine what Uncle Byron had to have paid for such a beautiful dress, let alone the cost of two dresses for her and Mariah. Before she could put it on, she went into the bathroom to begin her morning routine. She looked in the mirror and saw that the dark circles under her eyes had faded to a light shade of purple. A good night's sleep must have caused them to fade.

Fi brushed through her long hair and contemplated cutting it shorter, like Mariah's. It was a thought she had at least once a week but knew she could never bring herself to do it. The hair fell into her face, almost blocking her view of the mirror. She was tempted to put it into the braid she wore daily around the farm. The tight back braid allowed her to do her work without having to worry about it getting in the way.

Today, however, was a special occasion, and she knew a simple braid was not going to work. She took extra time to create two small braids at the top of her head and bring them around to meet in the back. The majority of her hair remained down while the front stayed out of her face. From many years of being in a braid, her hair had a natural wave to it. The waves flowed and cascaded all the way down to her waist.

As Fi made her way back to her room to put on the dress, she noticed Mariah coming out of her room to take her turn in the bathroom. Fi went to say good morning and apologize to her, but Mariah glared and went into the bathroom, slamming the door behind her. She thought Mariah must still be angry and hurt from the night before. But she decided to address it later when everyone was more awake and willing to listen.

When she entered her room, she shut the door quietly behind

her. She walked over to the bed and picked up the dress. It was soft cotton that would breathe easily on a warm day like they had been having. She pulled off the clothes she had slept in and tossed them in the corner. After applying her ointment, she donned a new pair of undergarments she had and proceeded to put on the dress.

The dress was best stepped into so as to not ruin the hairstyle she had just created. It fit like it was made for her. Almost as if someone came in and took her measurements, and then went off and made the dress. The waist was tight enough to flatter what little curves she had yet was loose enough she could easily move. The cut of the neckline lent that the illusion she had fuller breasts than she truly did. The hemline hit right at her ankles so there would be no dragging on the ground.

Once she was dressed, she looked for a pair of shoes that would go with the dress. Many of her shoes were covered in manure or mud from the farm. She didn't have a habit of keeping any nice shoes since they would never get worn. She tore through her room, looking for something she could use. Thrown under her bed, she found a pair of simple tan shoes she had long forgotten about. They were flat and barely came up over her foot. They matched well with the dress, and she placed the shoes on her feet and went downstairs for breakfast.

On her way out of the room, she heard Mariah talking to herself in the bathroom. It wasn't uncommon for Mariah to sing when she was alone. Mariah had a beautiful voice but never let anyone hear it. Her confidence was so low she hid every part of herself away, it seemed. Fi couldn't carry a tune in a bucket. She didn't want to be rude but couldn't help but to try to make out what Mariah said. The door, however, was so thick all she could pick up was Mariah was angry still. That should make for a lovely day at the festival.

Downstairs, Uncle Byron was in the kitchen, dressed in his best brown pants, only worn on nice occasions, and a cream-colored doublet with a dark blue vest over top. Uncle Byron was a handsome man, and many women had tried to gain his attention. But since his wife, Claira, passed, Byron never seemed to hold interest with anyone. He was busy getting all the dried meats and eggs together to take to town.

"That dress looks lovely on you," Byron said. His face looked up from the tasks he worked on. "Dorothy at the Dress Shop was right to pick that color for you."

"Thank you very much for the dress," she said back, smiling. "You really didn't have to spend the money on this for me." Fi knew money could get very tight around the farm, and this was an extra expense.

"Please, do not worry about it. It is not every day I get to spoil my girls," Byron said, beaming back. Fi loved when Uncle Byron called her and Mariah his girls. "Money is not something I want you worrying about. If I didn't have the money, I wouldn't have done it. Now, get something to eat while I finish getting everything ready to go into the wagon. He turned back around, putting items into more crates.

Their counters and table had crates and baskets full of food. There was dried beef and chicken, as well as many crates of eggs. Some crates held vegetables and melon from the garden, including broccoli, cucumbers, mushrooms, and two crates of watermelon.

"I thought we were only providing beef and eggs for the festival. Why do we have chicken and produce?" Fi asked.

"Mr. Porter's crops didn't come in as great this year, so I offered to help him with his portion of the festival," Uncle

Byron answered over his shoulder. "We have to help our neighbors as much as we can. That's how we survive around here. Takes a village they say."

That is Uncle Byron for you. That man would give someone the shirt off his back if they were in need.

Fi often wondered if her father was the same sort of man. She had never known him and was never told his name. Was he a caring and giving man? She knew he and her mother had a string of time together, and thus she was born. Her mother had given her up, but did her father know about her? When she was younger, she often dreamed a sweet and caring man would show up at the door, claiming he was not aware of her. Prove to her that she was truly wanted, no matter what her mother had done.

But no one ever came. The older she got, the more she let that dream go. She had already felt wanted and loved at the farm. She had Uncle Byron and Mariah for her family. It wasn't the same, but there were many who had less than she did.

Fi skirted around her uncle and the boxes to fry herself up some eggs. The pans for the stove were thankfully stored on her side of the kitchen. Putting the pan on the wood stove, she warmed it up and cracked two eggs. It was hard to make them over easy, as she preferred with such little space. Every time she would try to flip one, her elbow would bump Uncle Byron or a crate and the yolk broke. She gave up and decided to scramble them instead.

With no place to sit and eat in the kitchen or at the table, Fi went and sat on the couch to eat her eggs. She was thankful she scrambled the eggs since, when she dropped pieces, she did not ruin her dress. She walked back to the kitchen when she was done and washed her dishes. The cool water turned warm after only a few minutes. The wood stove must have been stoked earlier this morning. She had to pull the sleeves up on her dress to keep them from getting wet. When she finished washing the dishes, she returned them to the cupboards.

As she came out of the kitchen, Mariah was just coming down the stairs. She wore a deep hunter-green dress that made her blue eyes pop. Her sleeves were plain and did not have the extra loop for her finger like Fi's had. The neckline was squarer and pronounced than Fi's dress. Then again, Mariah had more of a chest than Fi could ever hope for. There was a simple black band going around the waist rather than a stringed belt.

Mariah's hair looked as it did every day, hanging straight down to her shoulders, with a small braid at her bangs pinned into her hair. As Fi's did yesterday, Mariah had deep angry bags under her eyes. Something kept her up last night.

"Good morning, Mariah," Fi said. "The pan should still be warm from the eggs I made if you want to use it." She didn't know how Mariah was going to be towards her this morning. After what she said last night, and Mariah's attitude this morning, it seemed as though it would be a day they should have spent apart.

"Thanks," was all Mariah said as she strode past. She had to have woken up in a bad mood or cranky from lack of sleep because there was no way that one comment could have led to this much anger. Fi had said harsher things in the past and was never met with this much contempt.

Instead of dwelling on it, Fi made her way to the back door to help her uncle load the wagon. As she opened the door, she almost ran into Erlan. He wore standard elvish woods clothes. A green tunic that tied at the top, and brown leather pants that were tucked into leather boots to help keep bugs and snakes from going up his pants. They were form-fitting and appeared tailor-made to his body.

"Oh, good morning, Fi," Erlan said, smiling at her. "Wow, that dress looks beautiful on you." Fi felt her face grow warm. Her heart sped up, and she thought it would leap right out of her chest.

"T-thanks," she stuttered. "Uncle Byron gave it to me this morning for the festival." She felt like a fool standing in front of him, getting wrapped up in her emotions. "I should probably help get the wagon loaded up."

"Of course. I came in to grab more to load. Excuse me." He moved past her, his body brushing lightly against hers through the doorway. Her heart skipped a beat, and her breath caught when they touched. His body just barely touched hers, but her whole body registered it. It lasted a matter of seconds, and she was outside. She was thankful his back was to her so he could not see her face.

Her burning cheeks were met with a nice, cool breeze. Her hair danced around her body, which reminded her why it was rare she wore her hair down. The sun was just above the horizon, so it was yet to be hot, but the mugginess from the night before remained. It looked as though there would be clouds in the sky today, which would help keep the sun at bay.

Crates and baskets had been brought out of the house that needed to be put in the wagon. Their wagon was old, just like most of the things on the farm. The wheels had been replaced and repaired multiple times. The frame and main body of the wagon were still in good shape. She knew it would have to literally be run into the ground before Uncle Byron would replace it.

There was not going to be enough seating for everyone, so two people would have to ride in back with crates while the other two sat up in the seat behind the horses. Fi hoped she didn't have to sit with Mariah.

She looked for the items that could safely be on the bottom and began loading them. Some were quite heavy and required more effort to get in by herself. She wondered if maybe she should have put on her dress after getting the items loaded. Erlan would offer assistance from time to time, but she would only accept if she truly needed his help. Once all the items to be taken were outside, it did not take long to get it packed up.

When Mariah finally came out, she was pleased she did not have to do any of the loading herself. One of the hardest parts was out of the way already. Mariah double-checked everything was in place and ready to go. She had a tendency to go behind Fi, like she didn't know what she was doing. As if she was still a child who needed guidance. Anytime she caught Fi's eyes, she frowned, and she would look away.

"I will go get the horses," Fi said finally. "After we get them hooked up, we should be ready to go." She turned before Mariah could protest and headed towards the barn. Fi had walked the path to the barn so many times that, even in the dim light, she knew the best way to get there. She contemplated staying in the barn for a bit but thought better of it.

The barn was still relatively dark, so she lit the lanterns. Opening the doors, she walked over to the equipment and grabbed two bridles and leads. She looked for the horse harnesses for the wagon but noticed they were missing. Uncle Byron or Erlan must have grabbed them earlier this morning. She snatched Hero's and Molly's bridles.

Molly was a quarter bay like the other horses in the barn.

She had stockings on all her legs that came almost all the way up. Her long black mane lay like a coarse blanket over her neck. She had burs caught in her tail, Fi thought she should remember to remove later. Molly allowed Fi to put the bridle on with no issue. Hero, however, was being stubborn and did not want to open his mouth.

"Fine, then I will just take another horse with me, then and you can stay here," she said over her shoulder as she went to put his bridle away. Hero protested and stomped his foot as she tried to walk away. "Oh, now you want to come with me, you pain in the ass." She walked back over, and he took the bridle willingly.

She walked out of the barn, taking a breath of air that didn't smell of horse and manure. Leading a horse in each hand, Fi started back to the house to get them hitched up. She felt a small pain in her right shoulder blade, but it quickly faded. She stopped so suddenly the horses almost pulled her over when they walked past. Fi put Hero's lead in her right hand with Molly's. With her left, she reached under her dress to feel her shoulder blade.

It felt smooth except for a few raises. They almost felt like she had been bitten by an insect. Being so near the barn, there was a strong likelihood she had been bitten by a horse fly. With the festival today, she did not want to cause any issues, so she decided not to tell Uncle Byron about them. With what happened the previous evening, she didn't want a horse fly bite to be turned into something else.

Once back at the house, she handed Molly off to Uncle Byron, and she proceeded to get Hero hitched up. Just as she thought, the harnesses for the horses sat next to the wagon. If she was paying more attention this morning, she would have seen it there. She patted Hero on the shoulder as a strong gust came through, tussling his mane into her face. She spat out the hairs that stuck in her mouth, and Hero whinnied at her. Of course, he thought it was funny.

With the horses hitched, and all the food in the wagon, they were ready to head into town to set up for the festival. Uncle Byron sat in the front of the wagon and grabbed hold of the reins. Fi waited to see where Mariah chose to sit. Mariah, of course, took the more comfortable spot in front, alongside Uncle Byron. Fi did not mind where Mariah sat if she did not have to sit with her. Erlan arranged the crates, creating two chair-like spaces for them to sit on. When the wagon had been settled into, they made their way towards the road and traveled to town.

Fi's stomach had begun to grumble. There had been much done since breakfast, and she had worked up an appetite. Thankfully, Mariah had put together portions of biscuits and fruit for everyone. They ate in silence after the hustle of the morning. That was the way of the farm, though. It never seemed there was a moment to relax or just be. There was always something to be done or something that needed fixing.

The farm was not too far from town and would only take them about a thirty-minute ride to get there. The roads to town were not paved but made of packed reddish dirt from years of horses and wagons riding on them. It was not a smooth road, so the wagon would bump and jostle around. A few times, a crate or two tried to share Fi's seat. As the horses walked, they kicked up dirt the breeze blew to the side of the road. Every once in a while, a gust would bring the dirt up at them, causing them to cough.

The sun had begun its ascension into the sky. It was

midmorning now, and the heat was starting to creep into the day. As much as Fi loved the dress her uncle bought, she wished the sleeves were much shorter. She worried her arms would get warm while working and enjoying the festival. It had to be something she would have to work through if it happened.

The view from the road was a boring one. They passed fields from other farms where they grew wheat and corn. The corn was coming to an end of the season. The stalk's green lively color had been replaced with a brownish-yellow. They blew in the breeze, creating a rustling sound as they brushed against each other. The stalks were still so high you could not see what was on the other side of the fields. It created almost a golden wall on either side of the road.

Past the fields were open grasslands. Many farmers used lands such as these to graze herds of cattle or sheep for their farms. The grass always grew lush around Baydell, offering great grazing grounds. Fi had heard Ditrem's land was so fertile it was almost impossible to not have anything grow. As if the goddess herself had smiled upon it, granting it favor. Surrounding the fields were thick forests of pine, oak, and ash trees.

The trees grew close to each other and created dark shadows over any paths that had been created. As summer neared its end, the leaves had started to change in color. The bright green leaves gained hints of yellows and oranges. They seemed to change earlier and earlier each year. During the day, the sunlight would stream through, creating patches of light throughout the woods. At night, they were ominous and full of danger. It wasn't just the wild animals you had to fear.

Gnomes were a common problem, but they were more of a nuisance than dangerous. Goblins were another story. There were also demons and other monsters that lurked in the forests. There had even been a rumor someone in Adonia had seen an orc. Which was impossible since they have been extinct for over two hundred years.

Fiends lived in the thicket so many people kept their distance. Fiend was a word used to describe a creature unlike other unnatural beings. They were in a category all their own. They were only ever described as serpentine. No one could ever elaborate more or was willing to. However, if someone were to come across one alone, they were never heard from again.

Before the armies helped control the numbers, the Fiends were numerous. They came out of the trees to prey on nearby farms. Sadly, it wasn't only the livestock they would take. Many farmers reported family members as missing or dead. The forest gave off an eerie feeling of dread and fear. Farmers kept their fields a good distance from the forest even though the Fiend numbers had dwindled.

Fi never got those feelings from the forest. There was a want to explore that had called her to the forest when she was younger. She was maybe fourteen when she had gone in once, following deer paths she had found. It was peaceful, and she felt like she had belonged. The smell of mulch and moss, mixed with the feel of nature on her hands, brought her such delight. She was meant to be there and contemplated staying in the woods instead of returning home. Fi ended up staying out in the woods past sunset.

When Uncle Byron found her, she would never forget the mixture of anger and fear on his face when they had gotten back to the house. He explained to her all the dangers of the woods. She had to promise she would never wander into them again. Since that day, she never gave into the impulse to stay out that late again no matter how strong it was.

"So, once we get to town, we will have a designated spot for us to set up. We will need to organize so we can keep the food ready for those who are hungry," Byron said after a while. "The whole town is supposed to be at the festival, so we need to be ready for large numbers of people to want food."

While Baydell itself was a smaller town, it still had around twelve hundred people. That is a lot of mouths to feed in one day. Fi loved that Baydell was not very big. It allowed for a town to be able to come together when times were tough yet still have enough space and independence that everyone did not know each other's business if not welcome to it.

"Now, I will try to ensure you girls get time to enjoy the festival," Byron continued. "Just because we have to work and feed our neighbors does not mean you will be stuck there all day."

Fi was relieved to hear him say that. She had been excited for the festival when she first heard about it a few months back. Big things never seem to happen around Baydell.

The last *big* thing to happen to Baydell was the addition of another housing building. The city had a boom in families needing more space. The masons had to work quickly to erect the building from the ground up. But that was five years ago now and, since then, nothing interesting has happened. Twenty minutes before they reached the city, Fi decided to take a short nap. It beat staring at the wall of corn the whole time. Before long, they could see the stone buildings of Baydell. Erlan gently woke Fi as they got closer.

"Fi, we are almost there.," he said softly into her ear. Caught off guard, she jumped up, almost hitting him in the face. With quick reflexes, he was able to move out of the way in time.

"Sorry! You just startled me," Fi apologized, readjusting herself. She had a small kink in her neck from lying awkwardly across the crates. When she looked at the crate she had been resting on, she saw a small pool of liquid. She had drooled in her sleep. As she wiped her mouth with her hand, she realized Erlan saw her slobbering like a fool while she slept.

"It's okay. I am sorry I startled you. I just wanted you to have a chance to wake up enough before we got into the city," he said, smiling at her, suddenly amused. "That, and I thought you might want to clean yourself up a little," he spoke the last part to her in a whisper so as no one else would hear. He gave her a quick wink and sat back in the crates. Fi blushed and looked ahead towards the city they were about to enter.

The buildings were built entirely by the local masons. The brown bricks were held together by dark gray mortar that never looked even. Many had archways that would go over paths in the city, allowing for citizens to pass through them. Windows were kept at a minimum since they would always leak in cold during the winter months. This led to many homes and merchants using lanterns to see within the dwellings.

The roofs were made of burnt-orange terracotta shingles that slanted towards the ground to allow rain runoff. The roads were paved with gray stone but had a thin layer of brown dirt over them from travelers. There were trees throughout the interior of the town, creating small grassy areas for citizens to sit in and relax.

In the most northern part of town was the temple the religious folks would attend at least once a week. The top of the building came to a large peak at the top, with a stone sun carved into the side. By looking at the temple, it was apparent the masons took more time and care when building it. The beams lay even along the walls, and the mortar was regularly fixed if it cracked. The temple was the biggest building in Baydell. It was built large enough to house the entire town if everyone had shown up at once. On a good day, a quarter of the town would attend and praise the Goddess Edione.

Edione is said to be the great creator of life alongside her husband Ureus. The goddess was tall and beautiful. She was depicted as having long golden locks that hung straight to the ground. She had a perfectly oval face, and her blue eyes were large and doe-like. In every painting of her, she had cheeks with a pinkish tint against her pale skin.

Ureus was taller than his wife and just as beautiful. He was told to have hair as dark as coal that hung in waves to his shoulders. His almond-shaped, dark green eyes sat hard in his angular face. He was said to be as pale as Edione, as though they were cut from the same cloth. Unlike Edione's depictions, Ureus never smiled and seemed as though he was in a constant state of unrest.

Unfortunately, they both had different views on how the world should be handled. Edione loved her creations and wanted to make a beautiful place for them to live and prosper. She eyed her creations as any mother would lovingly look at her child.

Ureus, on the other hand, felt they needed to be controlled with a strict hand. If left to their own choices, the beauty they created would be destroyed. They could not be trusted with what he thought was precious. Angered by her husband's disdain towards the world they created together, Edione cast him away from her. She is said to be the sun giving light and hope, while Ureus is the moon cast into the darkness by Edione. As the priests tell it, Ureus still watches, waiting for Edione to see he was right, that their creations would turn on her.

In front of the temple was the town square. There were trees and a small pond that allowed those who needed to cool off to wipe their brow with clean cool water. Small fish swam around the pond, causing children delight. Benches were made of oak wood and placed around for citizens to relax and socialize. It also allowed the elderly to come out and watch the bustle of the town in peace. The temple would regularly clear the stones on the ground to free it from the dirt of travelers.

At the edge of the town square sat the schoolhouse. Many families did not send their children to school after they reached ten years old since they needed their help tending to family businesses and shops. Children tended to go to school just long enough to be able to read and write. The building was quaint, yet big enough to accommodate the small number of pupils it was going to need to teach. A new, painted sign hung above the door in a dark shade of green. For the entire school, there were two teachers to attend to all the students.

East of the temple was Baydell's local jail. Like the temple, it never had very many people in it at one time. Like the rest of the city, it was built with bricks of brown hues and dark gray mortar. The windows it did have had bars creating squares across the windows. There were wood shutters on the outside to place over them during the winter months. The jail had only six cell blocks inside to house any criminals.

Those who were charged with major crimes were normally sent off to one of the larger surrounding cities to be dealt with. Baydell's jail only housed those caught for petty crimes such as stealing. The sign above the door had long faded, and any unknowing passerby would not be able to tell that it was a jail unless they looked at the windows.

The housing area of Baydell lay south of the jail. Many of the buildings here were built together, creating communal dwellings. The stone walls were lined with oak doors and windows with winter shudders on each home. Every home had its own entrance and living quarters. The insides were simple, with wooden floors and beams on the ceilings. Their layouts were identical to each other. Everyone knew where to find something if they were to visit a friend.

Many buildings were two-level, offering families more space. Inside, the families had access to their own kitchens, bathrooms, and bedrooms. The main level would house the kitchen, a bathroom, and a small living space. Up the stairs would be three bedrooms. If a family had many children, they were better off trying to find a farmhouse that could house everyone more comfortably. Each building was large enough to house ten families. Throughout the housing district, there were thirteen buildings placed.

Located in the center of the housing was the community bathhouse. The mortar on the bathhouse had to be fixed regularly due to water damage from the inside. The building had hand pumps for water and, through taxes, the city provided wood for the citizens to stoke the fires for a warm bath. There were lines of baths that each had their own pump. There were small dividers between each bath, but many citizens did not feel uncomfortable bathing around everyone else.

One hundred people could bathe at one time. Due to this, each family had an allotted time slot in which they were able to use the bathhouse. Without the schedule, many families would occupy the space more often than others. This would not allow everyone a chance to clean themselves.

Not everyone was lucky enough to afford housing in multifamily buildings or a farm. This led to an area of town known as the Pit. If there was an area to avoid, the Pit would be that place. The Pit was known for housing shady individuals and known thieves. The buildings were rundown, and some were so decayed they were past the point of being habitable. The road was full of potholes, many areas unable to be traveled with a wagon or cart. Shifty business owners would set up shop to try and obtain customers of the same mindset. Illegal and stolen goods were often found in the Pit being sold off for coin.

The final area of Baydell was the marketplace. The road from the farm let right into an open square lined with shops and merchants. In the center, tents were being put up to house the city for the festival. While the market was always busy, there were never this many people in the market at once.

Although it was smaller, Baydell offered many options to purchase the items you needed. There was the produce shop called Perfect Nut, which would buy local farmers growth. The shop was run by Gale Scounce. He was a small man, maybe five-four and one-hundred-twenty-five pounds soaking wet. He had dark black hair starting to turn gray, and a pair of plain brown eyes. His nose was large and crooked in comparison to the rest of his face.

The Perfect Nut had bins set up out front, showing off the latest produce in season. It had melons, tomatoes, beets, berries of all kinds, corn, eggplants, potatoes, and more. Summer always had the best produce according to Fi. Inside, Gale sold seeds for farmers to plant on their farms and, in the far back, manure for those who did not have the means to make their own.

Next to the Perfect Nut sat the butcher shop. The Little

Hogg was run by Lawrence Hogg and his son Harold. Both men were heavy set with beady eyes. Lawrence's dirty blond hair was pulled back into a low ponytail, keeping it out of the way. Harold kept his hair shorter so there was no need to put it up. Lawrence's wife, Bonnie, worked the shop and helped to ring up customers. She was a small, frail woman, a striking contrast to her husband and son.

The Hoggs received their meat from farms such as Uncle Byron's. Some farmers would use them to butcher and package their meat for their families. Others would sell through the shop and split the money with Lawrence and Harold. There, you could purchase beef, chicken, and lamb. On occasion, they would also have duck and goose. The shop inside always had a strong smell to it from all the raw meat.

The blacksmith was next in the strip of shops. Lewin Page thought he was clever in naming his shop The Anvil. Lewin was a large man and had broad arms from manually making and fixing weapons, tools, and other odds and ends. At one point, he had short military-cut hair, but that was a thing of the past. He had a head as smooth as a newborn baby. That didn't stop him from growing a beard that put many to shame.

The Fletcher may have had another name at one point, but it had long been forgotten. Allen Branwhail was an average-sized man with bright green eyes. His red hair made him stand out from any crowd. His shop was smaller than many of the others in the market. He made arrows and fixed bows broken during hunting. He didn't always have a lot of business. When it was slow, he would apprentice under Lewin to further his weapon knowledge.

The general store sat on the opposite side of the square from the Perfect Nut. At the Iron Violet, one would find all their necessities. They carried local milk, eggs, flour, sugar, and household goods. It was an eclectic store that matched its owners, Daniel and Frances Driland. They were an odd couple who always looked like they were running late.

Their clothing never matched, and their brown hair was never combed. Frances wore large glasses on her face, making her blue eyes look larger than they were. They always had smiles on their faces and could brighten almost anyone's day.

The inn was a combination of sleeping space and a tavern. Lina Manston ran the inn, coined the Sand Man. Lina was a mousy woman and very quiet. She handled the thirty or so rooms they offered. There were three levels to the inn, and getting to the top rooms would easily make anyone want their bed. The rooms were currently booked from nearby farms, not wanting to make the ride home to their farms after the festival. Uncle Byron had reserved a room in case it got too late to take the horses home.

Leonard Manston was a stark contrast to his wife. He was not a muscular man, but he was not average, either. He was close to six feet and had a nasty temper. He ran the Dirty Kettle tavern connected to the Sand Man. Everyone in town knew that, if you got stupid, Leonard had no problem straightening you out. Many speculated that was why he opened a bar, so he could still fight from time to time.

The bakery was the best part of the entire market, in Fi's opinion. The smells that came out of the Common Cake could make your mouth water. Every day, Ellen and Hugh Cotton would bake fresh bread for the entire city. There was always a deal on day-old bread, which was almost the same. Ellen was a large woman with rosy cheeks and a head full of tight brown curls. Hugh was also built bigger but did not quite match his wife. The couple would also bake cookies, cakes, and pastries. Today, they bustled around, getting all the desserts ready for the festival.

The final shop in the market was the Dress Shop. The name was deceiving since they sold anything from dresses to pants to shirts. Dorothy Harte could even make perfectly tailored clothing for the right price. It was surprising her old eyes could see as well as they could. She had to be pushing sixty-five, but she had yet to slow down. Her gray hair was always perfectly pulled back into a tight bun, and she wore small round spectacles on the end of her nose. Fi thought she should thank her for picking out the dress she was given.

Beyond the market sat stables to board horses while people were shopping in town. There were individual stalls and simple poles to tie the horses to. A simple roof and walls protected them from the elements. A trough of clean water was refilled and available for horses to drink from. Hay was placed throughout in case the horses became hungry. There were already many horses housed while their masters were hard at work.

The family had finally reached their designated spot, which had been set up in the middle of the market square. There was a fairly large cart in which they could place out the food for people to come and eat. A small fire with a large skillet had been placed to cook the eggs and any undried meat brought over. A large canopy had thankfully been placed overtop, which blocked out the beating sun's rays. Uncle Byron brought the trailer to a stop behind the cart. He unhitched the horses, handing the reins off to Fi.

"Why don't you take Molly and Hero over to the stables," he told her. "We will start getting things set up here, and you can help us finish when you get back." Before she could answer, he turned from her and helped unload the wagon.

Fi happily took the horses towards the stables. She passed by the Sand Man and Dirty Kettle. She stopped for a moment outside the Common Cake and inhaled the smell of freshly baked goods. Her mouth watered at the smells wafting out the little front door. She understood why Mr. And Mrs. Cotton looked the way they did. She would, too, if she worked around such wonderfully delicious food.

As she passed the Dress Shop, she decided she would stop back by after dropping off the horses to talk to Dorothy. As the festival went on, she might not find another chance to do so. Oddly though, the sign in the window said *closed.* She had never known the shop to be closed before. Perhaps everyone already had their clothes. Dorothy may have been helping elsewhere in the festival. Fi would have to keep an eye out for her.

Fi finally reached the stables, and all the stalls were at capacity. Fi looked around to find a suitable place to tie up the horses. There was a hitching rail that had space near a bay with a white streak in its mane. The stable was slightly muggy from the heat, so Fi filled the water trough to its brim. Once she was satisfied, they were tied with a proper release knot, she headed back to the cart to help.

Much of the cart was already unloaded by the time she returned. Uncle Byron had taken the produce to Mr. Porter's cart. The crates and baskets had been separated to make the food easier to find when people came up. Much of the meat had been set out in front of the cart to allow people to grab whenever they were hungry. They just had to make sure it stayed stocked and eggs were cooked when needed.

CHAPTER 3

Banners were hung all over the market in deep greens and white, the colors of the country. Children ran with their toys and played tricks on each other. The city had come out to celebrate the marriage of their beloved king. It was set to be the best day Baydell had seen in a long time. It was supposed to be the best day Fi had seen in a long time.

Chapter 4

The festival had begun. The market was so full of people they bumped shoulders wherever they went. The only open area was a space designated for dancing, but even that was full. There were four maypoles at each corner, brandishing rich deep green and vibrant white ribbons that blew in the breeze. A band of instruments had set up on the far end and played a light, uplifting tune that would be easy to dance to. Easy for anyone who was not Fi, anyway. She had two left feet. She had planned on staying as far from the dance floor as she could.

Many of the citizens of Baydell had found their finest clothes to wear today. There were little girls with brand new ribbons in their hair, and little boys in their best dress. Ladies had long and beautiful dresses, and men wore pants and tunics. One could tell some townsfolk hadn't worn their dress clothes in a while. One man's stomach hung out the bottom of his tunic, and another woman's dress seemed stretched at the seams.

It appeared no one held back in what they had brought to share. Mr. Scounce brought out all the best fruits and vegetables for everyone to eat. The Hoggs were outside their shop with a pig still roasting on the fire. Many men could be found drinking at the Dirty Kettle, getting a bit rowdy. The cakes and pastries the Cottons made created such an inviting aroma it made anyone's mouth water.

Fi had kept an eye out for Dorothy of the Dress Shop, but she had not yet seen her. The cart they had been given was very busy. Many neighbors were hungry from dancing, walking around, or just trying to get through the crowd. The dried meats were eaten faster than eggs were being ordered. This did not surprise Fi since who wants hot eggs when the day had not held back its own heat.

Since the beef was self-serve, there was not much to be done. Mariah got to go and enjoy the festival first. Fi had thought to protest, but she decided otherwise. They needed space from each other and did not need any more drama. As Mariah slipped into the crowd, Fi sighed with relief. Without her there, it seemed as if a dark cloud that loomed over her had left. Something was off with Mariah, and Fi didn't know exactly what it was. She just felt as though it had something to do with her.

When Fi turned back towards the cart, she noticed the dried beef was running low, so she went to grab another crate to put in the current one's place. As she turned around, Fi hit something solid. In quick realization, she found the object was a person. Fi put down the crate and looked down at who she had hit. A young man lay on the ground, his shoulder-length deep brown, almost black, hair falling into his face. She recognized him as a man she had seen from time to time in town.

"I am so sorry. I did not see you there. Are you okay?" She offered him her hand to help him up. The man swiped her hand away as he tried to stand. Fi took a step back.

"Maybe you should look before you turn next time," he

sniped back, getting up without looking at her. He stood two inches taller than Fi. His chiseled olive face looked down, and his hazel eyes locked on hers. His face softened a bit when he saw who it was that hit him. A small smirk formed under his well-kept goatee. "I mean, yes, I am fine. Are you?"

"Of course, I am. I am not the one who got hit with a crate. Are you sure you are okay?" She looked him over, making sure she did not seriously injure him. He was a man of medium build. He was not as lean as Erlan but did not appear to have a large amount of muscle like Uncle Byron. He appeared to be a perfect combination of the two. His broad shoulders sloped into a fit waist, leading Fi to believe he had more muscle than his clothing let on. She quickly moved her eyes back to his face when she realized she had been staring.

"Yes, yes, I am fine." He did not seem to notice she had looked him over. He helped her move the crate out where people would have access to it. At this point, Uncle Byron had noticed Fi talking to the young man and made his way over.

"Need something, Iam?" Byron asked in an assertive yet pleasant voice. His body language gave off the need for protection. Fi had a feeling he had not come over to see if Iam needed food.

"Good afternoon, Byron," Iam said with a smile. "I was just apologizing to this young lady for bumping into her." His eyes flicked over to her quickly. "I am sorry I did not catch your name."

"It's Fi," she said, not realizing her heart had sped a bit when he smiled at her. "And really, it was all my fault. I need to pay better attention."

"No, it was mine. I should have been watching where I was going. Hard to get around in a crowd this big. I am the one who should pay better attention," he responded, gesturing around them. "I should leave you so you can attend the cart. Maybe I will see you later if you can step away." He offered one last smile and disappeared into the crowd. Uncle Byron and Fi walked back behind the cart to tend to customers.

"Who was that?" Fi asked her uncle. Even though she had seen Iam around, she did not know who he was. Up until now, she had not even known his name.

"That is the last of the Pine family, Iam," he responded. "You remember hearing about the farm in the west that burned down? He is the sole survivor of the fire. It is a sad story, really."

Everyone in Baydell knew about the farm that caught fire seventeen years ago. It was a cool fall night when a neighbor saw smoke and flames coming from the Pine's farmhouse. He had rushed over as fast as he could, but by the time he got there, the house was engulfed in a torrent of fire. There was nothing he could do for Mr. and Mrs. Pine, who were trapped inside. Upon reaching the house, the neighbor noticed a little boy sat on the front porch, crying and covered in ash. No one knows how he survived.

There were many stories about how the fire started. Some say a Fiend came out of the forest, and the house caught on fire while it was attacking. Others say Mr. Pine caught his wife lying with another man, and while lost in rage, set the whole house on fire. Of course, no one knew for sure what happened since the only witness was a two-year-old boy.

How sad and lonely he must have felt growing up alone, not knowing what had happened. Fi could relate to that feeling. She knew all too well what it was like not to know the truth about one's parents. To sit and wonder what might have been.

Thankfully for Fi, she had an uncle who took her in and cared for her. Poor Iam did not have that luxury. He was sent to a group home in Baydell to be raised until he was old enough to be on his own.

"You okay, Fi?" Byron asked her. She looked up at him, coming out of her thoughts. Her feet had stopped moving as if her brain used all its power to control her contemplating.

"Huh, yeah, I'm fine. I guess hearing about Iam made me think of my parents," she responded without thinking. Fi saw Uncle Byron's face tighten at their mention. Anytime she brought up her parents, he became tense and uncomfortable. Almost as if he was ashamed of who they were. No matter how many times Fi asked about them, he always would change the subject. Now was not an exception.

"Fi, why don't you go and enjoy the festival," Byron finally said, his body relaxing. Fi glanced towards the cart and noticed Mariah was not back yet. It had only been a few hours since the start of the festival.

"I thought it was my turn to leave when Mariah came back? I couldn't just leave the cart to the two of you," Fi said, glancing over to the crowd of people taking dried meats and pushing their way through to get to the cart.

"Mariah will be back soon enough. I want to be sure you get time to enjoy the celebration. You take life too seriously sometimes. Today is supposed to be about having fun not working all day. Besides, who knows when you will be able to relax and enjoy yourself like this again," Byron explained, smiling.

Even though he seemed in good spirits, Fi couldn't help but feel guilty about leaving them. She glanced towards Erlan, filling egg orders, and he appeared to handle things well. And the crates weren't that hard to fill. She wanted to argue with Uncle Byron, but she got a sense she would lose.

"Okay, but I won't be gone long. I will walk around for a little and come back," Fi explained, holding up her hand when Uncle Byron tried to argue with her. She knew he was going to tell her to take her time and take in the whole festival. She felt too much guilt about leaving to enjoy herself. "But first, I will check on Hero and Molly. You know how horses can get neglected when people are preoccupied."

He knew all too well how bad horses can be forgotten. When they first got Hero, he came from a farm in Perrin. They went to go look at him after being told of the condition he was in. Uncle Byron was angry when he heard a young horse had been neglected. He thought there was no one worse than someone who abused those who could not help themselves. Nothing anyone told them could have prepared them for what they saw when they reached the farm.

As they pulled up, it was obvious it was not being properly tended to. The buildings had broken and rotten boards. The fields had long been over-grazed as the cows were not properly rotated. Some of the chickens had begun plucking their feathers out from the stress of their conditions. Fi wondered how someone could look at their farm and think these were acceptable conditions.

Hero's original owner met them outside the beat-up wood farmhouse. He looked as though he didn't even bother taking care of himself. His salt and pepper hair was long and matted, and he was missing over half his teeth. The smell that came off him was not something Fi could ever forget, even if she tried.

They were led to the horse barn, and in the first stall was a sad-looking Palomino colt. The floors looked as though they hadn't been mucked in weeks. He was so emaciated Fi could count every rib. Upon closer inspection, she saw his hooves had not been ferried in quite some time. The bottoms of his hooves were long and cracked open. He was a sad sight to see.

When Uncle Byron asked why he was in that condition, the farmer said he bought him for breeding but found out that the colt was sterile. This was most likely due to inbreeding from the farm he was purchased from. The farmer had no use for him, so he stopped tending to him.

They took the horse home that night. The farmer had never really named him and just called him Horse. Fi picked out the name Hero for him after they got him to his new home. Uncle Byron and Fi worked for months with rehabilitation to get him to like being brushed and groomed, let alone ridden. Even now, Hero only liked Byron, Erlan, and Fi. Fi always took extra time to ensure he was cared for when she could. She would never let him be neglected again.

"Okay, but do not spend all day there. Please, get out and enjoy yourself a little," Byron called after her. He seemed desperate for her to break away from what she would normally be doing.

It was tough to make her way through the crowd. Everyone was packed so tight together she had to squeeze between people. The effort caused her stomach to beg for nourishment. She made to stop at the Hoggs's shop for a bit of roasted pig. As she got closer, however, the line was longer than she wanted to stand in. Fi decided after checking on the horses she would stop at a cart with a shorter line. Before the end of the festival, however, she would try their sought-after cuisine.

Fi tried to follow where the crowd thinned out. Around the shops and carts seemed to be the congregating places. This brought her zigzagging through the crowd. She had hoped to be at the stables already but had made it barely halfway. Soon she found herself by the bakery.

In front of the bakery, the crowd was impossible to go through. Everyone appeared to want one of the delicious pastries Fi smelled earlier, taking the horses to the stable. Her stomach grumbled, and she remembered again she hadn't eaten since the ride in this morning. That was the first thing she was going to do after she checked on Hero.

Since she couldn't go through the crowd, she would have to follow it down until it was thin enough to pass as she had been doing. The line of people was long, and Fi wondered how much further she would have to walk out of her way. Suddenly, the crowd stopped, and Fi felt relief until she realized why. The cluster of people had brought her to the dance floor, the one place she wanted to avoid.

The dance floor made an almost perfect square in the middle of the festival. The stones laid on the ground were flat and smooth. Someone must have cleaned them that morning since they had minimal dirt compared to the paths around it. In the square, couples danced, laughing if one made a misstep.

Children flocked together, doing what they called *dancing*. To Fi, it looked like jumping around and flailing their bodies. Before anyone could get her to dance, she attempted to skirt around and slip back into the crowd. Before she could, she felt a gentle tug on her arm.

"May I have this dance?" a familiar voice asked. Her head spun around to see who it was that wanted to risk their life dancing with her. Iam stood with his hand barely touching her arm, waiting for a response.

"Trust me, you don't want to dance with me. I am a terrible

dancer," she answered. "I am sure there are much better partners than me who would dance with you." He smiled coyly down at her as he took both of her hands in his and pulled her onto the dance floor.

"There is no such thing as a bad dancer if you have the right partner," he said cockily. He then pulled her feet onto his and twirled with her around the dance floor. The breeze created sent Fi's hair around them wildly. Her heart pounded, and she wasn't sure if it was from the dancing or being this close to Iam.

For the first time, she realized how dancing was supposed to feel. It was graceful and beautiful. Iam's feet synchronized with the song and moved at all the right moments. When the song ended, Iam returned her to her feet. They moved off to the side while the next song kicked up.

"See, I told you anyone can dance." Iam held onto her. Their hands fit perfectly together.

"No, you danced. I just crushed your feet while you did all the graceful footwork," Fi said, smiling up at him. "Thanks for the dance, but I need to be heading to the stables." He released her hand, and the warmth of it slowly left her.

"Why are you heading to the stables? You are not leaving already, are you?" Iam asked her, looking like a boy whose mother came to pick up his playmate early.

"No, I'm not leaving. I want to check on my horse and make sure he is okay. I get nervous leaving other people to watch him," she answered back quicker than she intended to.

"Oh," Iam's face relaxed, "in that case, let me escort you. It would be much easier to get through this crowd with me pushing through ahead of you."

"Why would you want to do that for me?" Fi asked. His eyes

sparkled as he looked at her, and her heart sped up again.

"What can I say, I have a soft spot for a girl who cares about her horse," Iam replied. "Besides, my horse is at the stables, too, and it couldn't hurt to check on her." She couldn't say no to him as he looked longingly into her eyes.

"Fine, just don't get too close to my horse. Hero is not a fan of strangers, especially men," she said over her shoulder as she began walking back into the crowd.

Iam quickened his pace and walked a step or two ahead. The crowd parted easier for him than it did for her. She was thankful he had offered to come along. Once past the bakery, the crowd was much less dense, and they were able to walk side by side. As she watched him, she could tell he was shortening his stride. Without her, he may have been able to make it to the stables already.

They passed the dress shop, and Fi noticed it was still closed. It was unusual for the shop, but Fi knew that today there wasn't much need for clothing that hadn't already been purchased. She told herself she was worried for nothing.

"Everything okay?" Iam asked, pulling Fi's attention from Dorothy. As Fi cleared her head, she realized she had stopped walking in front of the Dress Shop.

"Yeah, I'm fine," Fi answered, shrugging her shoulders. "I have a bad habit of getting lost in my head and apparently forgetting how to walk." Without another word, Fi continued towards the stables. Iam quickly followed.

"Can I ask what you were thinking so hard about?" Iam asked as he caught up to her. His face showed not only curiosity but what looked like worry. "It must take something important to make someone stop dead in their tracks." Fi tucked a piece of hair that had come free from her braid behind her ear.

"Nothing really," Fi said, looking at the ground. Iam grabbed her hand again, creating a warm feeling through her. Any unease she felt about Dorothy left her thoughts. She felt silly for worrying about something so trivial. Being with Iam gave her a sense of ease she had never felt before. She looked up at him, and he stared at her intently. Her heart jumped when she met his eyes.

"Well then, let's get going to the stables. We are just about there," Iam said, pulling her along. She had to move her feet quickly to keep up with his stride. They were like two children running together, playing. After a few minutes, they reached the stables, and Iam let go of her hand. Her hand held on to the residual warmth of his.

As they approached the stables, they could see most of the horses had been moved under the overhangs to give them relief from the sun. If Fi had to guess, there were at least twenty horses there. It wasn't hard to find Hero as he was the only Palomino. Fi walked over to him and patted his neck. He turned and nuzzled her gently. He seemed happy to see her.

Iam petted a bay Fi saw earlier, which had sock markings on the front two legs and stocking marks on the back. In the horse's mane was a single strip of white hair. The horse seemed calm under Iam's touch.

"This is Ithil," Iam said calmly over his shoulder. "She is really the only thing I can call mine." Ithil continued to chew on the hay.

"She is a beautiful horse, Iam. Ithil is an unusual name for a horse. How did you come up with that?" Fi asked, curious as to what Ithil meant. To her, it sounded foreign, as if it was another language.

"The mark in her mane makes a crescent shape when she

runs. I was fascinated by it the first time I got her into a gallop. I knew she needed a name as special as she was. Ithil means moon in Elvish. With the shape in her mane, it only made sense." Iam smiled as he petted the side of her head.

Fi smiled at him and turned back to continue giving Hero attention. With her thoughts no longer preoccupied, she realized she was alone with a man she did not know. Heat rose in her face. First, she was alone with Erlan, and now Iam. Why was this suddenly happening to her? She couldn't bring herself to turn and look at him, so she continued to pet Hero's neck and pulled a few burrs out of his mane.

"He really is a beautiful horse," Iam said quietly. Fi hadn't realized he had walked up behind her. Her breath caught, but she quickly regained her composure. Hero's ears moved backward with Iam's presence so close. "He really doesn't like strangers, does he?"

"No, he doesn't. He really only behaves for my uncle, Erlan, and myself," Fi explained as she tensed up. "Mariah cannot get too close or he gets aggressive. It's not his fault, though. With his past, I am surprised he trusts at all."

Iam must have moved a bit closer because Hero took a step to the side.

"Why do you say that? Horses generally love people unless they have been mishandled," Iam said with a touch of sadness in his voice. It was as if he already knew the answer to the question. Even though he spoke quietly, she heard him as though he stood right behind her. Her body became covered in goosebumps.

"Yeah, his previous owner did not care for him. The state he was in was horrible. Even the thought of it makes me sick," Fi said, looking at the ground. She did not want to cry in front of Iam, but the image of Hero in her head was unbearable.

Suddenly, Fi felt Iam's hand on her shoulder. When he made contact, her emotions calmed. *What is this effect he has that makes me so calm?* She turned around to look at him and saw his eyes watered as well.

"That is horrible to hear. What kind of person could do that to an animal?" Iam said. As he spoke, he made to move closer to her. Or maybe it was to Hero. Either way, he was coming too close. "At least he has someone to care for him now."

Iam slowly lifted his hand and moved to move a few strands of hair from her face. As his hand drew closer, however, he stopped himself. He seemed to realize he was about to cross a line. Fi could not help but blush.

"You know, you are really pretty when you blush," Iam said.

Fi's head swam. She was alone in a secluded place with a man she just met. If he had moved any closer, they would be in an embrace. She made a single step backwards to create a gap.

"I am not blushing, it is just really warm in here," Fi responded, trying to calm her thoughts. She took another step backward, and her back touched Hero's shoulder. Thoughts of Erlan entered her head, and she felt guilt. Even though Erlan never showed any reciprocating feelings towards her, she still felt like she was betraying him somehow.

"It is really muggy in here," Iam said, seeming to accept her reasoning. "Did you want to step outside and get some fresh air? The horses seem to be in a better state now."

"Yeah, sure. That sounds like a good idea," Fi replied. Not only would Fi be happy to escape the heat of the stable, but it would be more open and less intimate outside. Iam gestured for her to walk out the door first. She moved past him, ensuring their bodies did not touch.

Once outside, Fi took a big breath of fresh air. Guilt washed over her, knowing the horses were trapped in such a muggy environment and could not partake in the breeze. Her hair rustled as a gust of wind came through. More strands of hair worked their way into her face again. Fi regretted wearing her hair down. Iam stepped out of the stables after her. He, too, seemed to take in a breath of fresh air. He glanced back in at the horses.

"I, uh, should be getting back to my family's cart. I'm sure Erlan isn't enough help for my uncle right now," FI said. At saying Erlan's name, she felt a pang of disgrace and looked down and the dirt-covered stone.

"I think they can handle themselves. But I understand you want to get back to them. Hopefully, I will see you again, Fi," Iam said. He then turned and disappeared into the crowd.

Fi stood there for a moment, frozen, unable to understand how she felt. Her emotions were a jumble, and none of it made sense. She had known Erlan her entire life, and it only made sense the feelings she had for him were so strong. But here was a man she'd known for only a couple of hours, and he had sent her heart fluttering all around her chest. She sat on a nearby bench, trying to calm her thoughts.

As the minutes passed, Fi was finally able to collect herself enough to make her way back to the cart. The crowd was harder to push through without Iam with her. As she neared the bakery, her stomach grumbled. It reminded her that she had not eaten since they had been on the road to Baydell that morning.

While the line to the bakery was long, the smells were intoxicating. She feared she would never taste the wonderful sweets the Cottons had prepared. Giving up on the bakery, Fi turned away and walked until the mass of people thinned.

The line was not as dense as it had been previously. This could be due to the townsfolk getting their fill earlier, or that it was closer to lunch. Around this time, many people would want something hardier and filling, like cured meat. At the thought, she picked up her pace back to the cart. She hadn't even thought about what time the cart would become busiest. It had been a bit since she left, and she didn't even know when Mariah was set to return.

Fi received many disgruntled looks from people as she shoved them aside. It was rude to push harder than needed to get through crowds. At that point, Fi was no longer concerned with being polite as her family needed her. She never should have left the cart. Not only was it not her turn to leave, but if Mariah came back and saw her gone, she would be even angrier with Fi. Sweat beaded on Fi's forehead, not only from the heat but also the exertion of pushing and running.

The cart was finally in sight, and a mass of people clamored for food. She picked up her pace, almost tripping on the hem of her dress. Her breath was coming hard. Trying to move quickly in a dress was proving difficult. From now on, Fi vowed she would never wear a dress again unless she was not going to be moving at all. Hair escaped from behind her ears in larger amounts. They stuck to her sweat covered face. She tried to wipe them off only to have them replaced with more hair sticking.

The closer she got, the more she could smell the meats, and her stomach reminded her how empty it was. Erlan was busily cooking eggs as fast as he could while Uncle Byron and Mariah bustled to get new crates of meat out for the townsfolk.

Unfortunately, Mariah caught sight of Fi first and made her way over to her.

"Where the hell have you been? I came back to the cart a little early to be nice, only to find out you had left already. So, not only did my time get cut short, but I have been picking up your slack!" Mariah's face was scrunched into an ugly scowl that almost made Fi not want to answer for fear of setting her off more.

"I had no idea this would happen. And Uncle Byron was the one who told me to go and enjoy the festival before you got back. I argued with him, but you know how he is when he has made his mind up on something," Fi attempted to explain. She did not match Mariah's volume as the townsfolk were already staring from Mariah's previous outburst.

"So, you go and blame someone else for your mistake. How perfect is that? Nothing can ever be your fault, can it, Fi? Whenever something doesn't go right, you always have a great way to explain how you didn't do it." Mariah's face glowed red. Her voice was shrill, and more and more people turned to look.

Fi had no idea where all this anger was coming from. To her knowledge, she hadn't done anything to deserve it. Uncle Byron finally realized where the commotion was coming from and made his way over in an attempt to break them up.

"Look, I didn't ask you to come back early. That was your choice. Which, by the way, I appreciate," Fi said, raising her voice a bit. It felt warmer than it had been a moment before. The heat of pushing through the crowd had nothing on what she felt now. "And how dare you try to put blame on me when there is none? Did you expect me to sit here and argue with Uncle Byron and still end up going, anyway? I don't get what your problem has been with me today, but lay off!"

The heat Fi felt shot out of her body, and a nearby cart caught fire. Their argument instantly stopped as everyone turned to stare at the flames. People rushed over to put it out and smother the cooking fire right next to them.

That is what must have caused the fire, Fi thought. Just a coincidence it happened when her body no longer felt like she was going to burn to death.

"What is going on?" Byron said under his breath as he grabbed both girls by the shoulder to let them know they were in trouble. As his hand made contact with her right shoulder blade, the pain she had felt the night before erupted. Only this time, there was no buildup, just a rush of pain that made her cry out in agony. Byron was able to catch her as she fell limp, passing out from the torment.

Chapter 5

When her eyes opened, Fi was in her bed with her blankets covering her from the neck down. Her body felt warm and sweaty from the air trapped against her skin. As she tried to move the covers off, her arms protested the change in position. Her bedding appeared to become heavier than the last time she had used them. As her body rolled to one side, her joints ached as if she had been lying in the same position for an extended period. Sitting up proved harder than it should have been.

She looked out the window and saw it to be just before dusk. When she fainted, they must have taken her back to the house to recover. Looking around the room, she caught sight of Erlan sleeping in the corner. He had brought his bedroll into her room and must have fallen asleep while waiting for her to wake up. While he slept, his face looked strained, as if he was carrying stress with him in his dreams. She didn't want to wake him, but the minute she went to stand, the floor creaked, and his eyes shot open.

"Fi, you're finally awake," he said as he jumped up and strode over to her. His eyes were wild, looking into hers, trying to ensure she was well. "We have been so worried since you fainted. Byron was losing hope you would wake up." Erlan reached his hand out and helped steady her. She felt weak and fatigued.

"Why would he think that? I have only been out for half a day?" Fi tried to ask nonchalantly, her tone more seeking reassurance it was truly only a short time. Her body implied she had been out longer, but she just couldn't believe it. She sat back down as her head became light. Erlan placed his hand on her back and supported her, helping her down.

"Actually, you have been unconscious for almost two weeks. We did not know how much longer we were going to be able to keep your body nourished," he explained. One never knows how a person will react knowing they lost two weeks of their life. Fi's eyes sprang wide. *Two weeks?* She had laid in that bed for two weeks with the two of them fighting to keep her alive.

"I-I don't understand. What happened to me?" Fi's words were barely audible as she sat on the bed, staring at the floor.

She tried to think back to the festival before she lost consciousness. She had been running through the crowd, breathing hard and sweating. She hadn't eaten anything for half the day, and then got in a fight with Mariah. It had to have been heatstroke enhanced by not eating. It was a perfectly rational explanation. It wasn't until then she remembered the pain she felt moments before the darkness.

She reached across her body to feel her shoulder blade. The bumps she had felt the weeks before had become what felt like some sort of design. Some areas were filled in while, in others, she only felt her own smooth skin. Erlan's hand met hers, and she looked into his eyes. They were filled with concern and sadness.

"There is much you must know, but I am not the one to tell you," Erlan said to her. "I will go and fetch Byron. He will be relieved to know you are awake and will want to speak with you." He broke contact with her and crossed the room to the door. He looked back over his shoulder before leaving. "No matter what, you are the same person you always have been. Don't forget that." He left without another word.

The last thing he said to her struck her hard. What did he mean by that? Was there something that could change who she was? She had so many questions and no one to give her answers. Her whole life turned upside down, and she didn't even know why. She felt alone and confused, like a child left behind without an explanation.

After a few minutes, Uncle Byron ran down the hallway. He burst into her bedroom with tears in his eyes. It was a sight she had never seen before. He had always been a stoic man, saving his smiles for the best occasions. It made them all the more special. But now, here he was, crying over her.

"Thank the goddess you are alright," he said. He sat on the bed next to her and threw his arms around her in an embrace. He gripped her tightly as if he was afraid at any moment she may slip away from him. When he finally released her tears were openly streaming from his eyes causing the blue to appear a crystal color.

"Of course, I am alright," she stated. Her brain refused to accept it was anything but severe sunstroke and exhaustion. "I just need to pay better attention to myself, is all. I am sorry to have worried you." His face hardened when he realized she did not understand. But how could she? She did not know her whole story.

"Fi, it was not the sun that caused you to faint." He took a deep breath, thinking about how to tell her the truth. "The mark on your shoulder blade was the cause of your unconsciousness, your Mark of Enchantment."

It took a minute for Fi to hear what he had just said. There was no way for her to have that mark and not know it, let alone still be in Baydell. She would have been hauled off at birth for Highbarrow. No, it didn't make sense.

"What are you talking about? If I had the mark, I would have been taken from here, or wherever it was my mother had me. If this is a sick joke, it isn't funny." She looked into his face, hoping, praying he would crack a smile and tell her it was just a story, and everything was fine. His face, however, did not change. They sat in silence for a few minutes before Uncle Byron began speaking again.

"Fi, I am about to tell you the truth of how you were born and how you came to live here. First, I want to say I am sorry for never telling you earlier. I thought the longer I kept it from you, the safer you would be. I was wrong, and I fear it has now made your life harder. I hope after this, you can find a way to forgive me." His eyes dropped to the ground in shame, and Fi waited to hear what he had to say.

"Your mother was beautiful. She looked a lot like you, so much so, in fact, at times, I swear you were the same person. Her pregnancy with you was easy as far as pregnancies go. She was so excited to meet you and add you to the family. I think your sister was jealous of the attention you were already receiving," Byron explained, a small twinkle in his eye as he spoke.

A sister? She had a sister and was never told about it? She wondered if her mother loved her that much, why had she given her away.

"Eventually, she accepted she was going to be a big sister and wanted to take on the role. Your mother was so proud of her for it. Life seemed perfect... until the day you were born. Things don't always go as planned, and no one was around when she went into labor. She was out doing chores when you decided you wanted into the world. She was brave and found a place in the barn that would provide both safety and comfort to you both until someone came home. But there were complications..." Byron's voice caught, and he had to stop a moment. He took several big breaths, calming himself and controlling his emotions.

"When I got home, I found you in the barn wrapped in your mother's work apron for warmth. You were sleeping peacefully on her chest, and I thought she was asleep, too. As I got closer, I was struck by the truth. While I was gone, Claira died alone holding you, trying to keep you warm." Upon hearing that name, Fi's brain put pieces together. Her thoughts swirled as they assembled the truth. Claira was Uncle Byron's late wife, but how could she have died holding Fi? Was she not Uncle Byron's niece, but his daughter? He realized she had understood what he told her. Byron calmly waited to see how Fi reacted.

"I am not Fi Silvera but Fi Summerheld?" Fi paused for a moment, mulling over what she had just asked. "If I am your daughter, why did you lie to me all these years? Did you blame me for my mother's death?" she asked, snarling. She did not understand why all the lies and secrecy. She should not be blamed for an act out of her control. It still did not make sense.

"No, no, no. I never blamed you for what happened. How could I?" he answered quickly, reassuring her that was not the reason at all.

"Then why? Why keep me here yet lie about how I came to do so? I just don't understand." Her questions came out quicker, and tears streamed from her eyes.

"Fi, calm down and listen to me. Everything was to ensure your safety. You see, you were born with the Mark of Enchantment. And, as you know, that means you would be sent off to live in Highbarrow," Byron explained. She gave him a look conveying she still did not understand. "Before you were born, we were sent a letter from Sir Eiton Claymore. He was a knight serving up in Highbarrow but was originally from Baydell. His mother, Dorothy, and daughter, Alexandria, still lived here while he was at his duty post. It informed us of what was really happening behind those walls."

"What do you mean *the truth*? It is where a young wizard goes to attempt to control their powers, so they don't hurt anyone by accident," Fi stated. She thought back to the festival and the fire.

"That is the story spun to convince those to send their loved ones to Highbarrow and not blink if they do not return. Syler informed us that learning to harness the magic in their bodies was not always successful. As if their bodies rejected the magic they were born with. But according to Eiton's letter, this was not the truth. He did not know the full extent of it, but he knew what he saw." Byron stood up and walked over to the window, looking out at the farm, fists clenched.

"Eiton was walking his normal rounds when he saw a strange sight. Part of the wall was uneven and pushed in slightly from the rest of the bricks around it. As he approached, Syler spoke strangely to one of the young wizards he had seen around Highbarrow. He carefully peered in and saw him in a room with a young wizard with her wrists and ankles held tight to her body by what seemed to be nothing. Syler performed some sort of ritual, and a light was drawn from the girl, going into

Syler. The girl fell limp, and that is when Eiton realized the truth. Syler was not helping young wizards, he was killing them and stealing their power."

Fi's head felt like it was going to burst. Everything she thought she knew was a lie. She couldn't process it all, it too much. She laid back down on the bed, feeling sick, and put the pillow over her head. Its down softness covered her face, and Fi contemplated just staying that way. Even her bed felt wrong as if she was never meant to lay in it. Byron walked towards the bed and pulled the pillow off her face. She could see he had more to say but held up her hand.

"I get there is more to tell me, like how you hid the mark for so long. But, right now, I just want to be left alone. I don't know who I am anymore, and I can't handle any more information. And though I forgive you, I just don't want to look at you right now," she said, staring at the ceiling, not looking in his direction at all.

"I understand. I will be downstairs whenever you are ready to talk," Byron responded as he turned towards the door. He paused at the doorway as if he wanted to say more, but he started off again, footsteps fading down the hallway.

Fi laid motionless on her bed, trying to digest all Uncle Byron, her father, had just told her. How could he have lied to her for so long? Who else knew the secret of her birth? It was all too crazy to believe. She was hoping it was all a cruel and elaborate joke, but in her heart, she knew that was not the truth. She tried to move her body to sit up, but her body only rolled to the side and brought her legs up to her chest. Tears welled in her eyes, and she wept.

She cried for the life she wished she still had, and the years she never knew the truth. Her emotions swirled between sadness for herself, grief for a mother she had truly lost, guilt for years of hating her, and anger at Byron for deceiving her. The pillow beneath her grew wet and soaked her hair. Finally, Fi was able to stop the tears and stared at the wall, calming her breathing.

Her body allowed her to have control again at last. She did not know how long she had been in her bed since Byron left the room. Fi raised her hand and wiped away any remaining tears lingering around her swollen, sore eyes. Standing, she slowly made her way to the bathroom to try and clean herself up. As she reached the door, she peeked a head out to see if anyone was in the hallway. She heard voices downstairs but saw no one. Crossing the hallway quickly, she shut the door behind her.

Looking in the mirror, she saw she looked as awful as she felt. Her eyes were pink and puffy. The green irises seemed dull as if she cried out some of their pigment. Her nose reminded her of when she had a bad cold that past winter. It was red and runny. She poured some of the cold water into the basin and splashed her face. She hoped it would reduce the apparent signs she had been crying. Grabbing a small towel, she dried her face. The cold water did nothing to help her appearance, but it somehow made her feel better.

Turning her back to the mirror, she moved her hair over her left shoulder. She pulled down the right side of her shirt to get a better look at the mark. If it wasn't a sign of magic and trouble, it would have been beautiful. A straight line went down the middle, expanding on each end. A thin delicate line traced through its middle, creating a small curl going up on the right and down the left. If Fi didn't know any better, she would have thought it an elvish symbol.

With a loud sigh, Fi turned towards the bathroom door and slowly turned the handle. She found her whole body trembled. She wondered what more there could be to tell her. Did she even want to know the rest? Even though she may not have wanted to, she needed to. She could no longer exist within the lie she had been living. Opening the door, she stepped out and moved down the hallway.

As she neared the stairs, she saw a light coming from the living room and heard Byron and Mariah's voices. Gathering all the strength she could muster, she forced her feet to walk down the stairs. Every step brought her closer to the truth. It was not her uncle and cousin waiting for her, but her father and sister. The thought made her head spin, and she caught herself against the wall.

In the living room, Byron and Mariah were having a deep discussion by the fireplace. Erlan had sat on the couch furthest from them. He watched them intently, not wanting to disrupt whatever it was they were saying. A floorboard squeaked as she took a step, and everyone turned at looked at her. Mariah made eye contact and turned away abruptly.

"Fi, I was beginning to worry about you. How are you holding up?" Erlan asked her with concern in his eyes. He could easily see the obvious evidence of crying on her face. "I am sorry it is all coming out like this. It must be hard with everything thrown at you at once." Erlan shot a glance back at Byron and returned his eyes to Fi, trying to read her expression.

"I-I think I am doing okay. I still don't know how to feel about it all, if I am being honest. I just don't understand how it was kept from me for so long." Her eyes looked to Byron's, hurt crossing over them. "I don't mean how could you not have told me. How did you hide the mark?" The part of her that didn't want to know anymore tied up into a knot. Byron drew in a big breath.

"We used a bit of elven magic," Byron began.

"Wait! Elves have magic. I thought their magic was lost to them after the *unspeakable evil.* How is that even possible?" Fi's words poured out of her mouth. The more the truth came out, the more nothing made sense. Uncle Byron held up his hand to stop her from asking more.

"They do not technically have magic in the way you are thinking. Generations of elven shaman have passed down rituals and recipes for certain ailments. One of these was intended to use in times of war. It is almost a cloaking paste. When rubbed on the skin, it takes the form of whatever is around it. In your case, it was unmarked skin." Fi thought back to the ointment she had applied every morning since she could remember.

"So, when I was little, and you told me I was vulnerable to the sun, it was a lie to ensure the mark would stay hidden?" she couldn't help asking, even though she already knew the answer. So many lies had been told to her in her life.

"I am sorry for all the deception, Fi. It was the only way I knew to keep you safe. I would rather have lied to you than you die at the hands of Syler," Byron answered in a low voice. "I couldn't stand the thought of losing you as well as your mother." His eyes glazed over again, but he shook his head, stopping the tears.

Fi wanted to be angrier than she was. She wanted to hate him for all the years of lies and false feelings it created. She never had a chance to be who she may have been destined to be. However, he did everything out of love. To keep her safe, even if it meant putting himself in harm's way if the truth of his deception ever came out.

Anyone caught trying to hide a child with the mark was sentenced to death immediately. There is no trial. It is considered the worst offense someone can commit. And Byron took on that risk for her. So, as much as she wanted to hate him, she couldn't.

"I understand, but what do we do now that I can't hide the mark anymore?" she asked, curious if it would just require more care when dressing and being around those in town.

"Unfortunately, there is another problem besides your mark no longer being hidden," Erlan said, looking at the floor. Everyone turned to look at him. "Don't tell me I am the only one who noticed the flame that left Fi's hand, causing the cart to catch on fire."

Fi sat down on the couch opposite end of Erlan. She glanced at her hands, and they looked as they always have.

"No, you aren't. But, hopefully, we are the only ones who saw that. I am sure if someone had, we would have seen a guard by now with questions," Byron answered in a low voice.

"We were lucky this time, Byron. We may not be so lucky next time. Someone could see her magic, or worse, someone could be hurt by it." He quickly looked to Fi. "Unintentionally, of course. I know you would never hurt anyone on purpose."

Fi gave him a weak smile, unsure where that left her with the danger of her staying.

"So, what would you have us do? Cast her away, putting her in danger to protect the neighbors? No, I will not have her out alone and vulnerable. I have protected her, her entire life. That isn't going to change now." Byron stormed over to Erlan. Fi had done nothing wrong, and he couldn't protect her outside of the farm.

"I never said she would be alone, Byron," Erlan said, not reacting to the anger. "I would accompany her, of course. And there is another you know would follow if you were only to ask. But it is too dangerous for her to be in such a small town where anyone could see. And as you know, word spreads quickly in Baydell once a good bit of gossip starts." He lifted his eyes, meeting Byron's. With a sigh, Byron nodded in agreement.

Fi felt faint again. She had just begun processing the information she bore the mark and who she thought was her uncle was her father. Now, this new bit of information tried to overwhelm her brain again. She had to leave the only home she had ever known. The furthest she had traveled from the farm was Baydell.

"Where would I go?" she asked the biggest question in her mind. "If the mark is known everywhere, how I could possibly be safe anywhere?" She suddenly felt trapped in a world she would not be accepted in. Condemned for something she had no control over.

"There has always been that rumor," Mariah said quietly. Everyone turned to her since it had been the only thing she had said in a while. Truthfully, Fi had forgotten she was there. Everyone had a puzzled look on their face, not knowing what she was talking about. "Don't tell me no one listens to the gossip you were just talking about. There is a rumor a small band of wizards has started a community in Adonia. They have somehow managed to stay off the radar, and no one knows where they are. King Tranan, of Adonia, has always kept tight borders. What perfect country to hide in."?

Byron and Erlan looked at one another. They spoke without using words. Suddenly, Erlan stood up and excused himself.

He walked past the kitchen and out the back door. Fi watched the door, waiting for him to come back in, but he did not.

"Where did he go?" Fi finally asked. Her head continued to spin, trying to process the information she had learned in such a short amount of time. Her eyes felt heavy from crying, but she did not feel tired.

"He will be back. I needed him to run a quick errand for me. Do not worry, Fi, everything is okay," Byron told her.

"How can you sit there and continue to lie to her?" Mariah turned quickly from the fireplace to face her father. He seemed hurt and went to open his mouth, but Mariah cut him off. "You know what really angers me? For years, you not only lied to her, but you lied to me. The sister I thought I had lost was sleeping in the next room to me. And she is the only one you cared about lying to!" Tears welled in Mariah's eyes. Her cheeks turned pink.

"Mariah. I—" Byron tried to speak to her.

"No, you don't get to apologize now that I am standing here pointing it out to you. It just solidifies what I have always thought. I am first born and second pick. Since day one Fi has always been coddled and favored. She is the reason my mother is dead, and yet you still chose her! I wish you would have let her go to Highbarrow and let Syler take her!" She gasped as the last sentence left her mouth. It seemed she had not meant to say it, but the words were already out. Before anyone could say anything, she ran up the stairs and out of sight.

"Fi, she doesn't mean what she is saying. She is just hurt and angry about everything. But it is not your fault. This is on me. I should have trusted you girls a long time ago. I didn't want to believe Erlan and wanted to keep you safe. But now, we have to face the reality of what is ahead of us. I am sorry," Byron said, looking at the door Mariah had slammed behind her.

"So, what do I do now?" Fi asked, curious about what the next steps in her life were going to be.

"Now, you go upstairs and pack anything you might need. You are leaving Baydell tonight."

Chapter 6

In her room, Fi still tried to comprehend all the information. She didn't even think about what she should pack. Not until she looked down and saw her canvas traveling backpack was still empty. Shoving the overload temporarily out of her brain, she looked around her room, determining what she should take with her. It was then she realized she wasn't sure where she was exactly going. Was it going to be cold? Warm? This was impossible.

Ultimately, she decided to pack a little of everything. She went to open her trunk, and her heart sank. There had not been any time to clean her clothes. *Wonderful.*

But, to her surprise, all her clothing was clean and neatly folded in her trunk. Byron must have known it needed done and did it while she was unconscious. He really did take good care of her.

Before packing, she dressed for travel. She donned a pair of dark brown leather pants, a loose dark green long sleeve shirt, and pulled on her boots, ensuring her pants were tucked tightly into them. Opening her bag again, she grabbed pairs of brown cotton pants, short sleeve shirts, long sleeve shirts, undergarments, and the pair of flats she wore at the festival. At the bottom of her trunk sat the icy blue dress Byron had bought her. She could not think of a need she would have for it but couldn't help staring at it.

Pulling herself away, she walked over to her wardrobe and grabbed a towel and a very small pillow. Her bag had a special loop that held her bow on her back. Grabbing her bow, she placed it in the loop and a few arrows in another special pocket. She wanted to save some space in her bag for food but couldn't stop thinking about the dress. Fi walked back over to the trunk and picked up the dress. She placed it on the top of her bag and pulled the top over to buckle it. Finally, she attached the bedroll she used when hunting to the top of the backpack.

Fi threw the bag onto her back, realizing this was all she owned now. Taking one last look around her room, her heart ached. This might be the last time she would see this little room. She took one last walk around and ran her hand over her bed one more time. She tried to memorize the grains of the wooden floor and the coolness of the stone walls.

She crossed the hall into the bathroom and braided her hair down her back, securing it with a long piece of leather. She placed her hairbrush and extra leather strands into her bag. Looking in the mirror, she barely recognized herself. Who was she, really? This was a question that would not leave her mind, no matter how much she tried not to think about it.

She used to be so sure of herself, and now she had no idea who or what she was. The brightness she once held in her face had faded, and she looked like a shell of her old self. Her eyes had no gleam and were stale and lifeless. Even her hair appeared dull. She could no longer look at herself and made her way out of the bathroom.

Her hand ran down the walls, and she walked towards the stairs, attempting to lock every detail into her memory.

Pausing at the top of the stairs, she took a big breath in an attempt to prepare herself for what was to come. The first stair decided to creak as she placed her weight onto it. There was movement from the kitchen as she continued down. Byron was in the kitchen, putting together what looked like a sack of food. Next to it were apples and loaves of bread. He turned towards her as she got to the bottom of the stairs.

"Are you all packed and ready to go?" Byron looked up at her while he finished placing food in the sack. She wondered where she would store it. Her bag already felt heavier than it probably should have, and there was no room for anything else.

"Uh, yes, I think so, but—" She attempted to answer him, but he quickly cut her off after he heard her say yes.

"Good. Everyone is waiting for us down at the horse barn. We better get there quickly or we will lose your cover of darkness," he said in a rush and began walking towards the back door. He held the door open for her and waited for her to follow. "Fi, are you coming?" She didn't answer and followed him out the door into the crisp night.

Even though it was still summer, the brisk fall air was beginning to move in. It was a mostly cloudy sky, which made it hard for Fi to see the stars. It also meant the moon was mostly covered, and the walk to the barn would be a darker one. The forest was one giant shadow of trees that could easily hide Fiends stalking them. The darkness settled around them till she saw a burst of light next to her. Byron held up a lamp to help illuminate the way, even though both had the path memorized.

As they walked, Fi realized how heavy her pack was. She had camped well outside the forest while hunting before but had never carried this many supplies or clothing. She realized then she had made a mistake trying to pack for any circumstance she may have come across. It would have been smarter to pack the bare essentials and purchase anything else she needed along the way.

Fi did not know what waited for her at the barn or who they were meeting. Once again, she was being swept into it all with little to no information. She tried to ask Byron questions, and he put his hand up silencing her. It was beginning to wear on her that she had no control anymore over anything she was doing.

Halfway to the barn, Fi caught movement at the forest edge to her right. It looked too small to be a Fiend she would have recognized, not that she had seen one. If anything, it looked human. But who would be lurking in the woods, following them? She stopped and stared, her eyes straining, trying to see any movement. The shadows in the forest, however, remained still. Her eyes must have been playing tricks on her.

"Fi, everything okay?" Byron whispered into her ear, making her jump.

"Yeah, I thought I saw something moving over in the trees," she explained to him, returning her gaze to where she had thought she caught movement a moment ago. It still lay motionless.

"It is most likely a Fiend. We had better hurry to the barn," he said, taking her hand and quickening his pace. She had a hard time keeping up with his strides but kept her balance. It reminded her of when Iam pulled her through the festival to reach the stables. For some reason, she was sad for leaving him behind and not seeing him again. She quickly shook off the thought. Feeling ridiculous, she was sad over a man she knew a few hours.

By the time they reached the barn, Fi breathed hard and had begun to sweat. In order to keep up with Byron's long strides, she had to keep to a light jog. He shot her an apologetic look as he placed his hands on the old barn door. He slid the doors open to reveal the lanterns had been lit, and a few people stood inside.

The lanterns cast a dim light around the barn. There was just enough light in the middle to make out everyone. The first face she spotted was Erlan's. His eyes were soft as he looked towards her. A look of concern crossed his face as her body tensed from nerves. She quickly looked at the other faces she recognized.

To the right of Erlan was Dorothy Harte. After the story Byron had told her about Eiton, she wasn't entirely surprised to see her there. She was dressed in what looked like white nightclothes, with a green robe thrown over the top. Her gray hair lay over her shoulders and was a lot longer than Fi would have thought. Dorothy gave Fi a slight smile as their eyes met.

A tall young woman stood just behind Dorothy. She appeared to be older than Fi. If Fi made a guess she was closer to her late twenties. Her features were striking, however. Fiery red hair was brought back into a loose, low ponytail. Some strands of hair wisped around her face. Her large eyes were stern and reminded Fi of the soil in the earth, with their rich hickory color. The woman bore light armor and, on it, Fi spied the mark of the Soeric Knights. This must be Alexandria, Dorothy's granddaughter, daughter to Sir Eiton.

A man leaned on one of the stable walls. It was darker there, so Fi strained a little to see who it was. Realization crossed her mind. It was Leonard Manston of the Dirty Kettle. She could not think of a single reason he would be here. Byron never had dealings with him as Byron didn't drink.

He, too, was in his night clothes. He wore a pair of gray cotton pants but had on no shirt. A stomach that showed he partook in his own product hung over the top of his pants. As Fi looked at those in the barn, she did not notice Byron had stopped walking and ran into him. She looked up, and he smiled.

"Sorry," Fi said.

"It's okay, Fi," Byron said to her softly. "There is a lot going on. It is a lot for a mind to process at once." He turned to face the four other people in the barn. They stopped any murmuring and gave him their undivided attention.

"Thank you for coming here tonight. I know it is late, so I will keep this brief. You were all trusted with the secret of Fi's mark. You have been loyal and have helped to ensure she was not taken to Highbarrow. But now, I fear that her magic has awoken, and she can no longer hide here in Baydell. We plan to move her out tonight so she may try to gain a hold of her powers on her own."

"And just where do you think she can go and hide, Byron?" Leonard asked. "Do you think there is a place in Abaddon she could go no one would register the mark if they saw it? Or not recognize magic should it escape her body again?" His eyes narrowed, and he appeared almost angry at Byron.

"As long as she keeps the mark hidden under clothing, she has a chance of going unnoticed. I would not want her going into large cities should she lose control. As to where she is to go, a possible place has been presented to us. There has been a rumor of a wizard refuge in Adonia. We will start there looking for the answers we need," Byron said, keeping his calm.

"Yes, let's trust the Adonians because they have always been so forthright and helpful in the past," Leonard snorted.

"Do you have a better idea, Leonard?" Dorothy said. "If you have any better ideas, by all means, share them with us. Otherwise, you can keep your worthless opinions to yourself." Leonard opened his mouth to say something and closed it again.

All of them. All of them knew this secret except her. She felt as though these five people had simply plucked out a piece of her life and locked it away. She tried not to feel angry. Tried to hold onto the bit they did it for her safety but, still, she couldn't help but feel robbed.

She stared at her feet, unable to look into the faces of those who had lied to her for years. The floor of the barn was a slight comfort. It was in this barn she had sought escape for years when she became angry or stressed. But now, there was no escape from what her life was.

"So, I must ask of you one more time," Byron continued, "please, offer what aid you can for her travels. Leonard—"

Leonard scoffed again, cutting him off.

"What is it you would want from me, Byron? I kept the secret all these years, so the bare minimum is required of me, in my opinion. In the end, I am not even sure I made the right decision. I would be lying if I said the thought of contacting Syler didn't cross my mind. I do not know why I even bothered to—" Before he could finish his sentence, Byron had him pressed up against the wall, riling the horse behind it. While the men were equal in height, Byron won in sheer size.

"Need I remind you, Leonard, that you were a brother to me. We shared everything until you ruined all of it. You made the choices you did, and I covered for you. The promise you made me was before you became someone I did not recognize. In return, I kept your secret. But don't think for a second our past allows you to threaten my daughter. You will keep your promises if you intend for me to keep mine." Byron's eyes were narrow and full of anger as he let go of Leonard. All Leonard could do was nod in agreement with Byron.

Watching the scene caused Fi's heart to sink. It was a side of Byron she had never seen before. It was terrifying how easily he could throw his weight around if he needed to. He walked back over to Fi and put a reassuring hand on her shoulder. He glanced around to see if anyone objected, and they all just looked at him with wide eyes.

"I offer my assistance, Byron," Erlan spoke out after a few minutes of silence. "I have traveled for many years and am familiar with many of the woods. I know elves are not always welcome around Abaddon, but I will accompany Fi wherever I can go." He placed his right hand over his heart and bowed. "I pledge my life to protect Fi." Her head whipped towards him as he spoke the last line. *His life?*

"I, too, will accompany her," said a voice Fi did not recognize. Alexandria stepped forward in front of her grandmother. "I will finish what my father started. I pledge my knight's oath to protect Fi." She dropped to one knee and placed her head on her sword. Fi had seen the knights take the oath before, but she had never thought it would be for her.

Although the fear of leaving should have been relieved with all the aid, she felt the opposite. Now, there were more people involved. More individuals whose lives would be changed because of her. She looked to the back of the barn in hopes of discovering a route of escape. If she ran fast enough and got out on her own, the only person truly affected would be her.

As she gazed at the far barn door, a hand settled on her back. Looking up, she saw Byron peering at her. The look on his face made it clear he understood what she felt. She relaxed, knowing any type of escape was moot.

"Please, then, ready your horses to leave at once. Too much time has passed already, and the sun will be rising soon," Byron said to all who accompanied Fi before looking at her. "Hero's bridle and saddle are already in his stall. He is greatly attached to you. Besides, without you here, I think he would become a useless, mischievous horse." Fi couldn't help but chuckle.

With a quick turn, she made her way back to Hero's stall. He seemed agitated by all the strange voices in the barn, and his brown eyes looked quickly to the stall door. The muscles on his back twitched with anxiety. His whole body relaxed, and sounds of happiness came from his throat as he realized who came in.

"Hey, boy," Fi said calmly, realizing his current condition. She did not want to cause him any more stress. Walking over, she fully saddled and bridled Hero. The minute her hand touched his neck, he relaxed. "It's time to go. I am not sure if we are coming back, but we have to go now." Knowing Hero wouldn't understand, she'd said it aloud, mainly for her herself. Making it more definite.

Fi walked Hero out of the stall and noticed only Byron remained. She was sure Erlan and Alexandria must have been outside with their horses. Making her way over to Byron, she noticed his eyes were glossed over from fighting back tears. Her heart suddenly felt heavy as the realization of leaving him behind set in. As angry as she wanted to be, this man was indeed her father. He could have given her up but, instead, changed his entire life to protect her.

Stopping right in front of him, Fi felt wetness running down her cheek. She lifted her hand and wiped tears overflowing from her eyes. Byron wrapped his large arms around her. As he embraced her, the dam in her eyes broke, and she sobbed. It was as if all her emotions from the night hit her all at once again. She couldn't help but lose control as she soaked Byron's shirt.

After a few minutes, she was finally able to gain control of herself again. Byron released her, and they stared at each other. There were so many things she wanted to ask him but, now, there was not any time.

"Please, take care of yourself, Fi," Byron said, his breath catching in his throat. "I hate how all of this has turned out, and it is my fault. I'm sorry—" Before he could speak anymore, Fi raised her hand and cut him off.

"You did all you could to protect me the only way a father could. Please, do not apologize anymore." She hugged him one more time before he could say anything else. "I love you, *Father*." Upon releasing him, she strode to the barn door, not able to turn back and look at him with fear she could not leave.

Chapter 7

As she thought, Erlan and Alexandria stood near their horses that were saddled and ready to leave. Alexandria's black mare, Zephyr, was large compared to Erlan's average bay stallion, Aranya. They blended much better into the darkness than Hero's coat did. Erlan caught the state of her face and quickly made his way over to her.

"Fi, are you okay?" he asked with a deep look of concern on his face. His hand rested on her shoulder, and she felt a familiar warmth where it touched. She wished everyone would stop asking her that. In truth, she was not okay. Nothing about her would ever be okay again.

"I'm fine, really. It is just a lot to deal with at once," was the only answer she could think to give. She placed her hand on his and forced a smile. "We should get going before the sun begins to rise." With much internal protest, she moved, allowing Erlan's hand to slide away. Placing her left foot in the stirrup, she easily mounted Hero.

Hesitating for a brief second, Erlan turned and followed suit, mounting his horse. Dorothy stood near them, talking softly with Alexandria, who was in a small disagreement with her grandmother. Seeing both Fi and Erlan ready to leave, they stopped whatever they were fighting about. Alexandria gave

Dorothy a weak hug and mounted her mare.

No more words were exchanged as Alexandria rode towards Baydell. Fi and Hero followed after, while Erlan took up the rear. Keeping her eyes to the ground did not change Fi, knowing exactly what she would be looking at. She had walked the land here enough to have it committed to memory. It wasn't until they came up to the house that Fi lifted her gaze.

Her heart caught as Mariah stood in her bedroom window, watching the procession of horses that carried away her sister. The sister she had always wanted but didn't know she had. The sister she, as far as Fi knew, hated her. As Mariah caught Fi looking, she turned her back and snuffed out the light. Fi held back tears, knowing it was not Mariah's fault for her feelings. She tried to imagine how things looked on her end and felt sympathy for her.

They traveled for ten minutes before taking a smaller dirt road to the right. This road led them right into the Lonrose Forest and away from Baydell. Fi looked around, not knowing what was happening as Hero followed Alexandria's horse obediently. The sun had still not risen, and going into the woods meant risking Fiends. Fi turned her head to talk with Erlan. He quickly put an index finger to his lips in silent explanation she needed to be quiet.

She stared at him, and he quickly whispered, "We are heading to the village of Pirn," He just as quickly fell silent. She returned her gaze to Alexandria, who seemed absorbed in the surroundings, apparently looking for dangers. Around them, Fi heard the familiar sound of owls hooting and leaves rustling from deer and other smaller creatures. With the animals in the area, there must not have been many Fiends. Silence was the only true warning.

Hearing the forest sounds was almost comforting. Fi closed her eyes and became lost in the noises of the forest. For a brief second, she forgot about the mark, about leaving home, not knowing what the future held for her. It was just a ride through the woods, and she longed for that brief reprieve to last. Sadly, she had to open her eyes to ensure Hero stayed on course with Alexandria. And, in an instant, her momentary escape vanished.

As they traveled down the road, the sky lightened and turned a pinkish-red in the eastern sky. From years of farming, Fi knew a sunrise of that color meant the following days should hold wet weather. If this was true, which it normally was, traveling would become miserable. If they had an exact location, they would be heading after the elven village it may not have been troublesome. But finding a place you do not know in rain and storm would be nearly impossible. It seemed as if the nature of the world aimed to work against her.

The areas between the trees became lighter, and she made out the shape of squirrels moving through the canopy. The wind seemed less in the trees than in their field, so the air did not hold the crisp scent of fall coming as it did the night before. She wondered how far it was they would have to travel to reach the small village of Pirn.

Erlan made this travel every few months alone. Then again, he would leave in the early mornings, so she had no idea how long before nightfall he arrived. She thought how lonely the ride must have been to go solo. With no one to talk to or pass the time, the journey must have seemed long. It explained why he was so talkative and energetic when he arrived at the farm. She knew she would be happy to talk to almost anyone after who knows how many hours of solitude.

They traversed the winding road east, towards the brightening sky. The red had burned off, and a pale shade of blue emerged across the sky. As they traversed a fallen cedar tree, Alexandria's horse stopped. Fi was confused, and she looked around but did not see a village in sight. Alexandria stared behind her. Her brows furrowed together, allowing all the freckles to become one solid spot. She tried to calculate something she could not understand, with her hand ready on the hilt of her sword.

Turning to look behind her, Fi saw Erlan off his horse. Holding the reins, he scanned the woods slowly, observing every inch of the surrounding trees. His expression held a look Fi had never seen before. A normally easy face was hard, jaw clenched. His eyes were tight and narrow as they took in every detail, looking for something out of place. The muscles of his lean elvish body were contracted, ready to pounce the moment he needed to. While the sight was a frightening one, it also sent a strange feeling into the pit of Fi's stomach.

Minutes passed as no one moved and everyone waited. Finally, Erlan's body relaxed, and his jaw relaxed. A bead of sweat slowly made its way down his face and dripped off his chin.

"I'm sorry for the alarm," Erlan said, remounting his horse. "I could have sworn I saw something out in the woods. It had been moving in pace with us for some time, but I fear it must have been my mind playing tricks. I was prepared for an attack from it the past few hours though I must have been seeing things." As he said it, Fi noticed he was not fully relaxed. His eyes still held an edge to them. She wasn't fully convinced he was wrong about seeing something.

"We should continue quickly, just in case." Alexandria's voice was a shock to Fi. In the tension of watching Erlan, she had forgotten they had another in their party. Fi heeled Hero forward again as her eyes watched the forest.

Another hour's travel, and Fi was finally able to see the beginnings of what looked like a village. The trees looked older the farther they rode. While through the Lonrose Forest, small saplings were easily found trying to survive near a well-made dirt road. The farther they traveled, less and less of these saplings appeared. It was as if the trees that existed had no need to create more to replace them.

Many species of trees grew together in clusters. Fi could make out oaks, cedars, chestnut, and walnut trees. There were some she could not determine. The trees had a look of wildness to them. Their branches were curved and twisted together. It became difficult to determine where one tree began and another ended. Dark knots and holes were visible. The roots of the trees came up out of the ground like legs wanting to walk.

In the distance, the road changed. Where it had been only wide enough for a single horse much of the time, it was wider now. It could now allow them to walk all three side by side if they so choose to. Instead, Erlan moved to the front of the three. This arrangement only made sense, seeing as this was his village.

The closer they got, the more beautiful the village became. The dirt became more packed and worn down, causing less to swirl up around them. As before, the trees here had pulled their roots out of the ground. This time, however, large roots systems were large enough to make the elvish homes. It was as if the trees rose from the ground to supply the elves with shelter, the roots intricately intertwined, creating walls with openings for doors and windows. Each had its own unique features as no two trees were identical. Some roots spiraled around each other, creating the looks of a braid. Others were wider and had large dark knots. The trees grew organically, but the road ahead of them was bare, leading to smaller side roads.

They lined the large road and had smaller streets break off from them. Houses were made on these side streets as well. The erection of the trees mimicked that of the buildings in Baydell. From a rough count, Fi estimated at least forty dwellings existed.

The sun had risen higher in the sky, casting beams of light between the tree branches. Houses that were hit with the sun directly had a shimmer of morning dew. It cast a beautiful light and lent the image they were encrusted with gems. The canopy created a flowing shadow above them that danced in the slight breeze.

If Fi did not know what she was looking at was real, she would have thought it a picture in a fairy tale. All this time, she never knew Erlan came from such a beautiful place. She realized how little she really knew of him.

"How is this even possible?" Fi heard herself saying before she could stop herself.

"Elves have always been close with nature. It always seems to find a way to provide us with food and shelter should we not be able to possess it ourselves. My father says it is due to old magic, but that is just another story of our people as we, of course, do not possess true magic," Erlan said casually over his shoulder.

Movement caught Fi's eye, and she returned her gaze to the village in front of her. Elves were coming out of their homes now. They appeared wary of the strangers entering their village with Erlan. They all had elvish ears and slender build. The women appeared slightly shorter than the men as a standard. Their pale skin was almost identical to that of Erlan's.

Fi wondered if, unlike humans, elves did not have a range of skin tones. Were they all the same in that respect? Hair color, on the other hand, was not a standard. It ranged from pale blondes one could say were white, to browns so dark they could have been mistaken for black.

While she did not want to make eye contact initially, she thought it could be taken as rude to completely ignore them. Her eyes fell upon the elves in their doorways. Their almond-shaped eyes looked back at her, almost with a trace of fear behind them. She tried to smile at one couple, but the woman quickly shut her pale green eyes and moved back into the dwelling.

No one could blame their reactions after how elves were treated by most humans. There were mainly adults who had come to gaze upon them. Only a handful of children could be seen trying to catch sight of the newcomers. From talks with Erlan, Fi knew elves did not reproduce often as they lived for such long periods.

In the center of the village stood a collection of chestnut trees. The largest chestnut tree stood out in the forefront of the others. Its roots were wide, which must have made the inside large enough to hold a small gathering. Its branches were thick and gnarled. They bent in random directions, providing a bountiful amount of shade. The leaves danced of their own accord, bringing more life to the tree. It easily had to be over three hundred years old.

An elf who resembled Erlan stood outside the tree, awaiting their arrival. They stopped their horses and dismounted. Erlan walked over to the elf and placed his hand over his heart and bowed.

"Father, I have returned home. Things have happened how you predicted, and the time has come that I must leave, potentially for good." He rose and met his father's gaze. It became apparent the chestnut color of Erlan's hair was almost identical to the bark of the tree in front of them.

His father stood a good four inches shorter than his son, with the same chestnut brown hair, but it was longer, almost to his waist. There was an air to him Fi recognized as authority. Just who was Erlan's father in this village? His eyes flicked up to Fi and Alexandria, and then back to Erlan. With a nod, he turned on his heels and disappeared into the tree.

"We are to follow him inside. It will be easier for us all to talk without the prying ears of the village." His voice was barely audible and shook slightly. Then, just as his father had done, he disappeared into the opening of the chestnut tree. Alexandria waited for Fi to move, and they both followed him inside.

As she suspected, the inside of the root forged home was immense. The entire village would have been able to fit if need be. Granted, it would not be a comfortable situation, but it was impressive nonetheless. On the sides of the dwelling were organically-shaped windows. In the city of Baydell, all windows are the standard square shape even if they do not contain a pane of glass. The windows within the elvish home had no defined shape but were whatever space the roots grew around. The floor was well-packed dirt.

A wall of vines hung partway through the room. Erlan stood waiting for them before he pulled them back to reveal the area his father lived. The floor was dirt as it had been outside, and there was little furniture. A small wooden table and two chairs sat on the far side of the room near a pair of beds. The frames of the beds were intricately carved with elvish runes with what looked like mattresses of cloth that had been stuffed with some kind of soft moss.

Shelves holding old-looking books sat on the opposite side of the room. A fine layer of dust and dirt had settled over the shelving. They must not have been pulled and read often given the thickness of the dust. Fi noticed that, in front of a book on the top shelf, a clean line was apparent. The book that would have been in that spot was missing.

Erlan's father sat on the floor in the middle of the room. He eyed them as they walked through the vines. Fi could see his face better now that she was closer. His eyes were blue, similar to Erlan's, though they lacked the piercing feature his sons possessed. He did not seem to show his years on his face. There were no distinguishable wrinkles or age marks.

His oval face held no amusement or lightness as Erlan's did. It was not stern but held seriousness and, being this close, increased the feeling of authority she felt before. If she had not heard this was Erlan's father, she would have thought him a brother instead. He gestured for them to sit on the floor in front of them. Following the request, all three of them sat in a semi-circle in front of him.

"I am Anrhil Evervine, chief of Pirn," he stated clearly. "I of course know who you are Fi Silvera, but *you,* I do not know." He turned to Alexandria as he spoke the last. Fi did not hear what Alexandria had to say in response.

Fi tried to get a grasp on the fact that Erlan, her Erlan, was the son of an elven chief. She questioned her friendship with

Erlan. Did he withhold the information because he didn't trust her? Or was she that caught up in herself that she never even thought to ask more about him? Once they left the village, she made a promise to pay better attention to those around her. Especially Erlan.

"Fi? Are you okay?" Erlan's voice came from her left. She shook her head, and everyone was staring at her. Her face burned with embarrassment as she muttered she was just fine. Placing his hand on her shoulder, Fi felt comforted. His fathers' eyes tightened on the contact between the two of them and Erlan moved his hand back to his lap.

"It is time Fi heard the stories of our people and hear the prophecy she has been intertwined with," Anrhil said, keeping his eye on his son. He waited for his reaction. Erlan's fists clenched tightly together in his lap as his eyes made contact with his father's.

As the moments passed, the intensity seemed to escalate between the two of them. An unspoken argument appeared to take place as Fi and Alexandria watched. In the end, Erlan hung his head with his fists still clenched. Nodding his head, Anrhil turned to Fi, his eyes falling seriously on hers. He opened his mouth to speak but, before he could, a male elf with ashen blond hair burst through the vine wall.

"I'm sorry to interrupt, but we have an intruder in the village."

Chapter 8

The three of them shot off the ground in an instant. Fi's mind raced, trying to figure out who would be intruding on the village. She doubted it was some lost traveler as the village itself was so far from any human settlement. It couldn't have been a full attack, either, or the messenger would have spoken with much more urgency. Anrhil moved swiftly to the vine wall and disappeared. Erlan was quick on his father's heels, a look of anger in his eyes.

"Stay behind me." Alexandria put her hand on Fi's shoulder, pushing herself ahead. With a hand on her sword, they made their way together through the vines, across the great room, and out towards the commotion outside.

The elves of the village were in a circle around what must have been the trespassers. They spoke loudly to each other about how to handle them. They spoke quickly in elvish, and Fi had a hard time even beginning to understand them. Erlan had taught her some of his language, but she only understood a few words they spoke *pestal, thori, javel*: human, life, and death. The beautiful elvish faces looked terrifying, holding such anger and hatred behind them. For people who cherished life, they seemed so ready to end it.

It bothered Fi that this could be someone who innocently

walked into the village could be seen as guilty so quickly. She knew it was not her place to step into elvish matters, but she needed to be sure someone who did not deserve it was not punished. She slipped away from Alexandria's guard and into the crowd. She made her way through the elves towards the center to see who was there. The elves were so concerned with the events no one noticed her moving through them.

There was one man on his knees, held by each arm in the middle of the circle. Longer russet brown wavy hair, lay over his lowered face. Through the hair, Fi could see human ears and knew his outcome was not a bright one. The laws of Pirn were simple to humans. Unless directly invited, as she and Alexandria were, humans were not permitted within the village. The punishment was severe.

The man raised his face, and recognition crossed over Fi. It was then his face met hers and her heart stopped. Iam. Soft hazel eyes held fear as they looked around at the elves, not knowing they wanted his life. He seemed to be trying to find a way out of his impossible situation. Any time he moved, the elves tightened their grip on him.

Blood dripped from his mouth, and his right eye was bruised. It was apparent he had put up a fight when discovered by the elves. He smirked slightly towards her before coughing blood droplets, speckling the dirt in front of him. Her mind raced. What was he doing there?!

"Molaeli." Anrhil raised his hand and, at once, the entire village fell silent. The quiet was unnerving after the chaos moments before. They all turned their faces toward Anrhil, waiting for him to continue. Anrhil, however, had turned towards Iam. "What are you, a *pestal,* doing in this elven village?" His voice was strong and sure, demanding the answer

out of Iam.

"Would you believe me if I said I got lost in my travels?" Iam tried to smile up at Anrhil through the obvious pain and fear. His face may have looked innocent, but even Fi could see the lies in his eyes. She couldn't believe at a time like this he would add further insult and try to deceive the chief. "Would you punish a traveler simply for being human?"

"We are punished by your kind for being what we are. Your easy lies are further proof of the lack of respect for our people." Anger flared in the chief's eyes. They took on a hard edge, and Fi visibly shook. "You will be sentenced as many before you have for entering our village with ill intent…death."

"No!" Before Fi could stop herself, she ran out into the middle of the circle, putting herself between Anrhil and Iam. She stood there, arms outstretched to block the chief's view of Iam. With a look of anger, she turned towards the chief and Erlan. Her gaze was met with a blazing fury from Anrhil, and confusion mixed with concern from his son next to him. The chief took a step towards her, but she refused to budge. She felt a familiar feeling of something growing deep in her stomach. The same feeling she had at the festival when she argued with Mariah.

"Move aside, Fi Silvera. This is a matter that does not concern you." The chief tried to keep his voice steady, but she could hear the rage bubbling just beneath it. A human had already disrespected him with lies, and now another challenged his ruling. "This is my village, and I must do what is necessary to keep it safe."

"I mean no disrespect. I do not try to question the ways of the elves." She tried to backtrack. Not wanting things to escalate more while, at the same time, something pushed her.

A heat formed in her hand, and something danced within her palm. She did not look down to see the cause. Her eyes would not leave the chief's. Behind her, Iam's eyes grew wide, seeing magic right in front of him. "He is no threat to you."

"How can you be so certain? He, a *pestal,* was found lurking just outside our village. He fights against our people, leaving some injured. What can you say to make me think that death is not the right fate for him?"

Anrhil did not seem fazed as the others did by the appearance of the flames in her hand. While the circle of elves had taken a step back, Anrhil stood his ground. Many questions for Iam came into her head, but they would have to wait until later if she could save him. As her anger and determination to protect Iam grew, so did the intensity of the heat in her hand.

"I can say this because I know this man. While I do not know why he was near the village, would you not defend yourself if someone came out of the woods and attacked you? He had no way of knowing he would simply be brought before the chief. In his mind, he may have been fighting for his life. He was obviously not far off," she said, much firmer than she thought possible.

Although she used the term *know* loosely. Spending an afternoon with someone was not enough time to truly know someone. But if a little stretching of the truth would save his life, she would stretch it. A low mumbling came from the crowd around them. The chief's face looked as though he contemplated what she said. Whether it was that or the now two flaming hands in front of him was unknown.

Her eyes bored into the chief, keeping her arms in a protective manner. Listening, many of the elves were spoke, but she did not understand. Stealing her eyes from the chief for a brief moment, they fell on her party. Alexandria gave a disapproving look with fear behind it. Fi had stepped into a matter that was not hers and, even worse, used her magic she was supposed to keep hidden. Erlan's face was solely anywhere but Fi's face. He went out of his way to ensure his gaze would not meet hers.

He moved forward to his father, talking quietly in the elvish tongue. They spoke with each other back and forth, not quite arguing. Like back in the chief's dwelling, there was an intensity growing between the two of them. This time, however, it was the chief who broke eye contact with his son. Erlan had won whatever argument they had.

"The *pestal* will be spared this day. The responsibility of his further actions will fall to my son. Should he act in a malicious way towards our people, Erlan will receive the same punishment. When Erlan leaves, he must take the *pestal* with him and ensure he does not come back. Until he leaves, return to your homes, coming out only when necessary. Please, release him." He motioned to the elves who held Iam's arms. They let go, and he crumpled to the ground.

The burning feeling in Fi's hands died the minute Iam was released. Fi rushed over to him, kneeling and helping him sit up. She stole a quick glance at her hands where there was no trace of a flame there moments before. Watchful elves eyed them as they turned to return their homes on the chief's orders.

"Iam, are you okay? What are you doing here?" She quickly pulled his face up to meet hers to assess his injuries. The blood no longer trickled from his mouth but was drying in his goatee. The dark hairs crusted together where the blood had run down. Her gaze went up to his now swollen eye. Deep purples were already forming around it. He was covered in sweat, and his breath was coming hard.

"I-it's kind of a long story," he said between breaths. He placed one of his hands on her shoulder, and her stomach flipped as it had done back in the stables. "Thank you for saving me from my arrogance." He locked eyes with her, and a feeling of warmth spread through her chest.

She did not hear Erlan and Alexandria approach until Iam's eyes flicked just over her shoulder. Alexandria's face was hard as it usually was, her hickory eyes scanning around the village, not fully convinced the danger had passed. Erlan looked as he always had, although he still held a slight seriousness behind his eyes.

"We should bring him to my home and dress his wounds," Erlan said quietly through a clenched jaw, bending down to offer Iam a hand up.

Iam dismissed it and rose to his feet on his own, keeping eye contact with the elf. He was unsteady on his feet and accepted Erlan's help at the second offer of assistance. Turning back towards the large chestnut tree, Erlan made his way.

Instead of entering the chestnut, however, Erlan veered slightly right towards a smaller elm. The elm did not look as though it was as healthy as the other trees in the village. The great trunk was lined with marks showing signs of attack. Ugly slashes from swords and gouges from arrows had been driven into the trunk. Erlan did not seem like one to attack his own home or a living tree. She wondered who would have done something of this nature.

Approaching the house, Erlan stopped and ran his hand along the tree. The bark of the tree appeared to respond to his touch. As if the house recognized who lived in it, the leaves danced even though the air was still. The connection between elves and nature was mesmerizing. A door lay in the center of the raised roots, and Erlan pressed on a knot that opened the door.

The door swung inward, and Erlan helped Iam inside. The two women followed, and Fi closed the door behind them. The floors in the house were dirt like the chief's home. It was packed so tight that little moved as it was walked on. There were two windows on almost every wall, allowing natural light to flood in. The house did not hold any furniture. There were no bookshelves or tables. A comfortable place to sit wasn't apparent. The area on the left side of the house, designated as a kitchen, had dust on it. All except the water pump appeared to have been ever used.

Iam sat propped up against the wall, and Erlan made his way to the pump. After a few pumps, he was able to get come cool water to flow out. He looked around and seemed to realize he did not have any cloth to dampen and clean Iam's wounds. Remembering she had packed a couple of towels, Fi placed her bag on the ground, dug around for one, and walked over to Erlan.

"Here, use this," she said, offering the once cream towel that had taken on a dingy color with age and use. Fi had always saved the oldest towels for hunting trips in the past since it was never a tragedy if they were ruined. Erlan took the towel from her without a word or even a glance towards her. He wrung out the towel into a basin and made his way back over to Iam.

In all the years she had known Erlan, he was never cold to her, not once. No matter what she had done or how disappointed he was in her, he always at least spoke to her. She realized she must have really crossed a line this time. It wasn't hard to see what she had done wrong today. But she couldn't let Iam be killed, though he would need to tell her why he was in the first place.

Trying to ignore Erlan's coldness, she walked over to everyone else. Alexandria walked back and sat next to the door. She was not relaxed, and her body indicated she expected someone to barge in and attack against the chief's orders. The hilt of her sword slightly drawn for an easier pull. The towel had been handed to Iam for him to clean himself up while Erlan sat a few feet away, cross-legged on the floor. As Iam's eyes meet Fi's, they brightened.

"How about we say we are even for you hitting me with that crate?" Iam said. As he chuckled, he grabbed at his bruised ribs. His laughter quickly turned into a cough. The festival seemed ages ago now after everything that happened.

"You need to stop making jokes and rest. Here, let me help you clean your face." She kneeled and took the towel. She didn't realize her hands were clammy until the cool, wet cloth touched her skin.

As she wiped the blood, dirt, and sweat from his face, Fi took in features she had missed before. His jaw line was strong and angular, and she felt a square chin under his goatee. His cheekbones were higher and had more definition. His hair was still loose and kept falling back into his face. Fi made to tuck it behind his ear, and his hand enclosed on her wrist. Her eyes shot to his in confusion and shock.

"Joking aside, Fi, thank you for saving my life. I would never have made it out of that mess without you. How did you make those flames appear in your hand like that?" His hazel eyes appeared as if a dark green leaf had begun to turn brown autumn. The colors swirled together in his eye. The grip on Fi's wrist was firm but not threatening. She pulled it away as he asked about her magic.

“The real question is, what were you doing in Pirn in the first place.” Erlan stood up quickly. The anger returned to his face. His blue eyes holding a storm, ready to destroy anything in his path. His jaw was set, and his jawline was more prominent than normal. Fists were clenched and slowly raised as if ready for a fight. Fi was taken aback as she had never seen this side of Erlan. He was always carefree and forgiving. Now, he worried Fi as to what actions he was capable of.

“Whatever I say, I doubt you would believe me,” Iam replied, trying to rise to his feet. He struggled as he used the wall for support. His jaw clenched in pain as his wounds wore against him. Alexandria’s armor scraped together as she stood from her position near the door.

“I doubt you two should be starting a pissing match right now. Iam seems to be at a great disadvantage with being injured. And, Erlan, I really doubt you would like to upset Fi any more than she already is. I get we need answers, but I do not think this is the best method,” she said, walking in between the two of them.

Erlan’s eyes finally pulled from Iam and glanced down at Fi. She had never felt such fear from seeing him. His gaze had always brought up happy emotions but, now, seeing him, she wanted to hide. Wetness blurred the irises of her eyes, causing the green to gleam. The anger in his face almost melted away. It was replaced with guilt and embarrassment. Without a word, he excused himself and went out the front door.

“Are you okay, Fi?” Alexandria asked, turning to her. While her face was stoic, her voice was soft and sincere. Fi nodded, not knowing if she could form words. “Erlan will be back once he calms down. I’m sure he won’t go far as he is supposed to keep an eye on all of us. I'm going to sit back by the door if you need me." With a final glance between the two of them, she sat back down.

Fi stood up and walked over to the window across the room near the water pump. The village looked deserted as the elves kept to their homes as instructed. She glanced around, hoping to see Erlan, but he was nowhere in sight. Fi could not help feeling like her world continued to crumble around her.

Chapter 9

Fi used the time at the window to collect herself. Though Erlan's approach could not have been worse, they needed to know why Iam was in Prin. She knew his *I got lost traveling* story was false. Anybody who heard him tell it knew he was lying. Something wasn't right, and she could tell he was hiding something.

Turning on her heel, she made her way back to Iam. Sitting on the floor, she crossed her legs in front of him and stared into his eyes. The tension was suddenly strong before a question was even asked.

"Iam, why were you all the way out here in Pirn?" The words felt thick in her mouth, but there was no other way to ask. She searched his face, waiting for his answer, hoping he would be more honest with her than he had with the chief.

"I'm going to sound like a crazy stalker after I tell you the story," Iam said quietly, shifting his gaze downward. Fi went cold but waited without saying a word. She did not want any reason for him not to continue. With a sigh, Iam continued his story, "I heard about what happened at the festival. The whole town was talking about how you had fainted, and the fire started near your cart. Granted, I didn't realize until earlier today you started the fire. I kept waiting to hear you had recovered and were well. I couldn't help but feel somewhat guilty that you fainted seeing as I dragged you around the festival. After weeks of hearing you had not recovered, I decided I would visit your farm and check on you."

Iam broke off, seeming to lose his train of thought. His gaze shifted to the window behind him, and he took a few moments to collect his thoughts back together. When his face returned, he made solid eye contact again with Fi. The green swirls in the brown intensified, and she felt every ounce of attention she had shifted to him.

"I ran into some old trouble in the Pit before I could get out of town. But that's a story for another time. Unfortunately, it caused me to leave town much later than I wanted to. I ended up getting to your farm as it was getting dark. My plan was to camp out at your farm just in far enough not to draw the attention of any Fiends. However, as I was walking, I saw you and your uncle walking towards the barn. I had to dart back into the trees."

"It was you I saw last night! I thought my mind was playing tricks from the stress of everything." As she spoke, her blood turned to ice. She had begun to wonder what he had heard anything that night. It would not be smart to let on more until she knew exactly what it was, he knew. "So, what made you follow after we left the farm?"

Iam shifted uncomfortably before he continued.

"I would be lying if I didn't say I snuck in closer to the barn and eavesdropped. Not one of my proudest moments." His eyes shifted away from Fi again, as though he was too ashamed to even look upon her anymore. "I'm sorry, Fi. I heard everything. I don't know why, but I wanted to help protect you. I can't explain it no matter how hard I try. I followed you here to Pirn and planned on waiting in the forest until you continued. Unfortunately, elves were easily able to find me." He knew everything about her that she had just recently learned.

She sat there blankly staring, not knowing how to react. He had wanted to protect her so badly he left everything to follow them. Was willing to risk himself for whatever was needed. It didn't make sense to her. He barely knew her and yet was willing to do so much so soon. At the same time, causing more confusion, she felt happy he was there with her. As if a small weight had been lifted off her shoulders. No response came to her lips. Alexandria saved her from the stinging silence between them.

"If you know Fi's secret, then we have no choice but to bring you along with us. That is unless Fi has changed her mind on your death." Her deep eyes held no emotion. Fi wondered if Alexandria kept things bottled up or if her knight training truly ran any emotion dry from her.

"Of course, I haven't changed my mind," Fi answered quickly, rising to her feet. There was a taste of anger in her voice. What was with everyone willing to take a life so quickly?

"Then he will accompany us." The voice was not Alexandria's but Erlan's. He had come in through the door during Fi's outburst. His face had lost any anger it held before. If anything, it looked slightly saddened. "I apologize for my actions earlier. I do not know what came over me. Accept my deepest apologies." With a fist over his chest, Erlan bowed low to both Fi and Iam. Though clearly still in pain, Iam stood to meet eyes with Erlan.

"There is no need to apologize, really. If I were in your position, I would have been angry, too. I handled everything carelessly," Iam replied with ease. "I understand you wanting to protect your village and Fi." Upon saying her name, he placed his hands again on Fi's shoulder, sending the familiar warmth through her body. Though Erlan said nothing, there was a small twitch in his mouth and a tensing in his shoulders.

"My father wishes to speak with us," Erlan said quietly as he made his way back to the door and slipped out. Exchanging glances, everyone followed out of Erlan's home, back to the chief's old chestnut in the middle of the village.

More time had passed outside than Fi had realized. Upon entering the village, the sun was still lower in the sky, signifying early morning. The sun now was high in the sky, burning bright. The dark shadows of the trees were short, offering little covering from the light. Not a soul could be seen in the village as she looked around. Fi thought she saw glimpses of movement within the windows, but Pirn appeared deserted.

It took mere minutes to arrive at the chief's door. Erlan was nowhere in sight to open the door for them. She stepped forward and knocked on the door, taking a step back to wait. Moments later, an elf, which was not Erlan or Anrhil, opened the door.

They were caught off guard by the female elf's appearance. Where most elves had long hair, hers was cut short and sat spiked over her ears. The golden blonde was reminiscent of beams of sunlight streaming through the trees. Her skin was as soft and glowing as the other elves Fi had seen in the village. If Fi had to guess, the elf was an inch or two taller than she was.

The elf's face was slightly mousy, with small features giving a sense of innocence, which complemented her svelte body. She hesitated as her cerulean blue eyes looked over at the three humans resting on Iam. They narrowed on him, a sense of loathing filling the irises.

"Let them in, Selain," Erlan's voice said firmly from behind her. With a sigh, she opened the door for them. As she stood aside, Fi could see both Erlan and Anrhil standing over by the dividing wall, waiting for them enter.

"Please, come in. We have much we need to discuss," Anrhil said, stepping behind the vines Erlan had lifted and stepped into the personal quarters of the tree. Selain made her way towards Erlan, who still held the vines to the side, waiting for everything else.

As Selain passed him, her face turned towards him, lighting up. The light dimmed in her eyes as Erlan made no movement to return the gaze. Fi followed behind Selain, who turned just in time to see Erlan meet Fi's eyes. Her body stiffened slightly as she turned back towards Anrhil. Iam and Alexandria quickly followed behind and Erlan turned to follow, releasing the vines behind him.

Anrhil sat back on the middle of the floor as he had the first time they had entered his house. As they all entered the room, he gestured for them to sit with him on the floor. Creating a semi-circle around him, they sat, crossing their legs beneath them. Selain made a point to ensure she sat next to Erlan, but he paid her little attention. His eyes were locked on his father's face, whose gaze was locked on Fi.

"Thank you for meeting with me. I did not plan on having this meeting after the events that transpired today." His eyes darted quickly to Iam, and then back to Fi. "But the matter at hand is more important than a single *pestal*. We elders believe the oldest prophecy of our people is finally at hand."

"Father, do not start with that old prophecy again. You drill it into all our heads, but how many years have passed with no sign of it even being true. Many of the stories you tell us are just that, stories. You act as though they hold any merit. We need to be concerned now with Fi's safety," Erlan said through gritted teeth.

"Do not all stories have some basis in truth? I teach these stories because they are the history of our people. While you and everyone else believe them to be myths passed down, we elders have known the truth. Almost all the tales are true. The one containing the prophecy is the most important of all," Anrhil explained.

Erlan and Selain shifted uncomfortably, already knowing the story that chief referred to. Fi wondered how bad the story could truly be. Her world had already been turned upside down and shaken violently. The story they were about to hear could not cause it to be attacked any more. She had no idea how wrong she was.

"Over five thousand years ago, elves and humans would intermingle trading goods with one another. Many elven villages were sought after for their healing magic. Almost all illness and injuries could be cured by the elves. Their magic was bright and beautiful. Humans could not possess this magic, but some sought after it for themselves. They thought the elves were foolish to only use such a power for healing and mending.

It wasn't until a group of *pestal* made a decision and changed the course of the world as we knew it. They wanted the secret to magic and kidnapped an elder elf near the end of his lifespan. They kept him hostage in a cave, trying to obtain the answers they wanted. The poor elf did not have many answers for these evil *pestal.* It wasn't until his dying breath he revealed that, in the elven villages, the magic is passed on through death.

The men waited for the elf to die to obtain the magic that was supposed to leave his body, and they succeeded. As the elf died, a puff of purple left his body. In elven culture, those who were chosen to inherit the power would stand near the body as the magic goes into the next living vessel. The closest vessel was a man named Reule. As the magic entered him, a mark on his cheek appeared. It was later called the Mark of Enchantment.

Fi's hand slowly moved to her shoulder. It ached slightly as she thought about the elf tortured in order for it to be a part of her. While she was not the one who had committed the act, she felt shame for bearing the mark.

"Reule was the first human wizard on record," Anrhil continued. "He used his magic destructively, punishing those who had wronged him and taking what he pleased. As he sired children with women they bore the mark somewhere on their body. Over the years, human wizards appeared regularly. It was not as much a curse rather than a simple mutation. *Pestals,* however, should not have such powers. Destruction happened more and more as mercenaries and criminals recruited wizards for their aid. Even militaries sought-after wizards to boost their ranks.

"We knew something must be done. The elders sealed the magic away, which took away our magic as well. They did not want a repeat of what had already occurred. Our life spans shortened from two thousand years to a mere five hundred. Two runes were created, sealing the two sides of magic. We believe that one of the runes, Nulla, was touched by the man named Syler. This released destructive magic into the world, and the mark returned."

Everyone sat in silence as Anrhil finished talking. With her head swimming yet again, Fi closed her eyes. Her mark came from an egregious act against the very people who have watched over her. If she had the mark, that meant she was a descendant of Reule, even if very distantly. And if Syler would have never touched the rune, she could have been a normal woman and the world would have been as it had been for centuries.

"But he has done so many great things to help Abaddon," she heard Iam saying softly. "He stopped the *Delirious Blight* and the attacks from..." He didn't finish his sentence that would cast the elves into a bad light. Fi opened her eyes as Iam hung his head, clearly feeling ashamed for bringing it up in present company.

"We believe those events were set in motion by Syler himself. What better way to obtain the trust of an entire continent than by saving it twice? The elves behind the attacks did not look like any elves we had ever seen before. Their skin was ashen gray and almost all their hair was black as coal. Their true origins are unknown. And as for the *Delirious Blight*, how convenient he had a cure after many important people were lost."

"And we are supposed to stop him? If he is as powerful as you claim, how can anyone stand against him?" Alexandria spoke through a tight jaw. A small fire burned in her eyes.

"The only thing we have to go off is the prophecy left behind by those who sealed the magic.

In a time of peace, a bringer of turmoil will arise. They will have the power to turn friends against friends and families against themselves. Those once filled with light will be overcome by darkness. Chaos will come before a false sense of peace rests across the land. In order to stop their infectious spread, the light must be returned. The bringer of light will be marked by matriarchal loss.

"It is clear now Syler raised the darkness of the Nulla rune. We believe, Fi, you are the one to return the light. You must find the Calwa ruin and release the light magic inside. Only then will you have the power needed to stop him."

"Why? Why do you think it is me?" Fi asked. It didn't make any sense to her.

"Eiton's letter came mere days before your birth. The timing of a new young wizard with the loss of a mother could not be ignored. The only conclusion we could draw was that our prophecy was about you. You are the one we have been waiting for, Fi," Anrhil explained.

An icy chill ran through her body. In just a few days, she had information shoved onto her that had been kept from her for her entire life. The truth about her mother, her father, and her mark. Her entire life has been a lie. A sham in order to keep the biggest secret from her. And now, she was destined and prophesied to return light and virtue back to Abaddon. No, it was too much she couldn't handle it, not now.

Chapter 10

Before she could stop herself, Fi stood and made strides for the door. Her legs felt like they had been filled with lead. Every step was labored and almost painful, but she couldn't stop herself from moving them. She had to create distance, make space from everything. If only she could find somewhere to be alone, everything would be okay. Her brain couldn't think as it kept replaying the events of the last day repeatedly.

Behind her were sounds of others standing to either stop her or follow her, but she didn't care. She made no attempt to turn around to see who it was. If she were to look back, her body may have no longer allowed her to leave. No, she had to keep going. They would only try to talk her into staying, and she could not explain to them how they had the wrong person. They would not believe her.

Reaching the vine wall, she slowly pushed it aside, stepping through, allowing them to gently fall back into place. Her brain not even sensing the smooth vines touching her arms and falling away. Everything was happening out of her control. Slowly, she made her way to the door, the world around her becoming a haze. Her hand grabbed the knob, but she barely registered its hard wood surface as she turned to open it.

"Fi, where are you going?" A far distant voice called out to her. It seemed to come from a million miles away. She could not answer the voice, even if she wanted to. Pushing the door open, the outside air hit her senses, and she was temporarily jarred from her slowed state. Distance, she needed distance, and she broke into a hard run towards the forest.

The chief's tree was in the middle of the village, so Fi had to run past homes and elves to reach the woods. The paved streets all looked the same, not that knowing which street was which would help her. She kept running in the direction of the canopy. She could feel eyes looking out of their homes as a human woman, a *pestal,* streaked through their town as though Fiends were at her heels. Finally, she was able to see the tree line and her speed increased with new resolute.

She did not slow as the trees blurred past her, and she sprinted through the forest. Flashes of browns and greens flew past her with every stride. Everything looked the same, and she could not distinguish one tree from another. There was no set destination. All she knew is she couldn't bring herself to stop or slow down. If she did, she would have to face everything, and she didn't know if she could.

Low branches found her face and exposed arms, while brush met her legs They skimmed across her skin, leaving fresh cuts and scratches. Luckily, she wore her traveling pants, her legs saved from damage. Still, her legs continued to carry her as though running from a dangerous predator attempting to take her life. Her lungs burned as she tried to gain enough breath to keep her body going.

As her foot caught an upended root, she flew forward, landing on the forest floor. She laid there with her face in the dirt and covered in leaves she had disturbed. Her entire body felt numb and, at that point, she did not even care if she was injured. Thoughts swarmed her mind, and she could not make sense of it all. Images and conversations flashed over and over in her mind.

She remembered looking at pictures of her mother in Byron's home, thinking how it was strange she looked so much like an aunt she was not related to. Their eyes were almost identical, with their jade shade of green and almost doe-like shape. She didn't understand how all these years she didn't see it. She wanted to blame Byron, her father, but how could she? Her heart went back and forth with how she felt.

On top of that was her mark. She slowly moved her body, curling into a fetal position and pulled her hand up to reach her shoulder blade where the mark lay. She held magic in her body forcibly taken from the elves ages ago. It was a stolen power she knew nothing about. And now, she was expected to use it to stop Syler. The reason for magic returning to Abaddon. A powerful wizard with powers she could not even fathom. How? How was she supposed to be this person? How could she?

With her knees to her chest, Fi just laid there on the ground. Her body, too tired from running who knows how far. She could not even find the energy needed to sit up. Her body used everything in its attempt to escape. Tears built behind her eyes, but they would not break the surface. She was no hero. She couldn't do what it is they asked of her. There had to have been some kind of mistake.

The silence of the forest was almost suffocating. Hearing anything would have been something to pull her mind even temporarily from itself. As the shock of everything wore off, her true emotions sank in. She did not only feel overwhelmed but sorry for herself. Fi wondered why it had to be her that all this was shoved on. Of all the people who bore the mark, what made her so special?

Rational thoughts seeped into her head now that she was stationary. She had run in a random direction into a forest she did not know. She could not remember the path in which she took to the spot she currently lay. How was she supposed to find her way back when she regained the strength or will? If she was going to go back, that is. Erlan coming to find her was the only way for her to be found. His tracking skills were remarkable. It was a question of whether he would look.

She did not know how long she laid there wallowing in self-pity before she heard footsteps through the leaves. The sun was hidden behind the canopy, but it seemed as though the light had shifted. There were at least three different sets heading her way. Knowing who it had to be, she longed not to be alone. She attempted to get up and call back out to them, but her body stubbornly denied her requests.

"Fi! Fi, where are you?" Iam's voice ran clear through the forest. It was frantic in his attempt to gain a response from her. The worry was thick through his voice as he continued to call her, "Fi, please, answer me!" Her thoughts had been on Erlan finding her, Iam coming never crossed her mind. She opened her mouth to call out, but no voice came out. She was in such a state her body no longer worked.

"Her tracks lead this way, follow me." Erlan's voice was slightly calmer than Iam's, but Fi heard the worry in his voice. She had seen him angry in a way that in all her years of knowing him never existed and now the tones of worry were new. His words were rushed as though if he said them faster, he would find her more quickly.

The sound of the footsteps grew closer and closer until Fi saw them through the thick of the trees. They must have seen her as well as they ran her direction. Iam pushed past Erlan, catching him off guard. This allowed him to reach her first. He easily picked her off the ground and pulled her into his arms. Her head against his chest, his heart beat rapidly. The tears held back showered from her eyes as though there was a waterfall behind them.

Every emotion she had been feeling and holding back gripped her body at once. She could no longer deny, and her body was racked with hard sobs. Every muscle contracted as everything poured out through her eyes. Her voice returned, and she could hear the cries leaving her mouth. The other footsteps stopped a little way behind the two of them. Her wails echoed throughout the entire forest. She was sure the village of Pirn heard her having a breakdown.

After some time, her sobs turned into heaving as the pent-up emotions were finally expelled. Fi tried to catch her breath as she wiped her eyes with her sleeves. Her eyes were surrounded but large red circles that matched her nose. There were streaks through the dirt and blood on her face where the tears had run.

"Fi, are you okay?" his voice was strained as it left his mouth. It appeared he had been wanting to ask that the minute he picked her up. His muscles tightened as he awaited her reply. Fi thought about it for a moment before finding her voice to answer him.

"Physically, I am fine. But it is just too much. I am being asked for too much. I don't know what to do, Iam." The sound that came from her was raspy, and her throat hurt as she talked. A side effect of the emotional release she had moments before.

Realizing she was still firmly pressed into Iam, Fi slowly moved away to meet his gaze, staying in his arms. His was face had concern etched into every feature. Powerful hazel eyes searched her up and down as his slender fingers ran over the cuts on her face and arms. He pulled her back into himself, encircling her body into a strong embrace. He held her for a moment before speaking.

"Fi, you are not alone. I know secrets have been kept from you, and a burden has been placed on your shoulders. But you do not have to bear it all. I will be with you every step of the way. If there are answers to find, we shall do it together. Please, don't think it is all upon you." Iam released her from his arms, and Fi could see his eyes becoming glossy. Before she could answer, another voice spoke from behind them.

"I have promised Byron I would watch out for you," Erlan piped in assuredly. "But if you think that I would leave your side on this journey, you are wrong. I am here to protect you Fi, whether Byron had asked me or not." His eyes quickly shifted to Fi in Iam's arms, a hint of jealousy and challenge entering his face before softening and turning them back to Fi.

"I am also sworn to protect you and stop Syler. Even if I wasn't, I could not let him get away with what he has done to my father. I will protect you in any way I can." Alexandria stepped forward, doing her knight's bow again for Fi.

Fi's eyes drifted over all these people who had come to find her in the woods. Each one had their own reason for helping her, but it lifted a weight from her heart. She didn't have to figure everything for herself. While she was supposedly the one spoken of within the elven prophecy, it never said she would do it solo. Maybe there was a chance after all.

As Fi attempted to stand, her legs gave out. Her body was

still weak from her emotional run through the woods. Before she could hit the ground again, she felt her body become weightless. Iam had swiftly and effortlessly scooped her into his arms. His heart was still slightly accelerated, but not as much as it was when he found her.

"You have run far from the village, and your body is worn. I can carry you back so you can rest," Iam stated. Fatigue rushed over her as her emotions calmed. Her muscles ached with every movement. Iam turned his body back the direction they had come. Fi could clearly see Erlan eying Fi in Iam's arms. With a nimble turn, Erlan's back was to them, and he began making his way back to the village.

"Iam, thank you for coming after me," Fi said in a hushed voice, and she buried her head into his chest and before he could respond, she fell asleep.

When Fi awoke, she appeared to have been taken back to Erlan's home. Her eyes caught sight of his small kitchen, where a pitcher of water sat on the counter. Behind it was one of the windows on that wall. The sun's position indicating it was morning, still low in the sky.

As there was no bed, she laid on the floor with her pack under her head as a pillow. She attempted to move and sit up and was met with resistance. Not from any outside source but her body itself. As in the woods, her muscles spasmed with even the smallest of movements.

Movement came from nearby as someone noticed her waking up. Opening her eyes, she saw Alexandria getting to her feet and make her way over to her. Fi's eyes darted around the room, trying to see where Erlan or Iam were, but they were not to be seen.

"Looks like you are finally awake. Here, let me help you

sit up." Her voice was softer than it had been earlier in the day. As Alexandria helped move Fi's aching body into a sitting position, she wondered how much time had passed.

"H-How long was I out?" Fi questioned. The last time she fell unconscious, she had been out for weeks. Moving to a sitting position lessened some of the pain in her muscles. She glanced around again, not seeing either of the men.

"Just the night. The guys bickered most of the morning, so I sent them both out to clear their heads for a bit. They were starting to drive me up the wall. I am sure they will be back shortly." She realized what Fi was thinking. Fi just nodded back to her.

While she understood some of their reasons for not liking each other, it should not have caused more fighting. It was really her fault that Iam was there and Erlan had the punishment of overseeing him. Erlan always got along well with almost every human he had interacted with. She could not imagine his distaste since Iam did not come to the village with ill intent.

"What were they fighting about?" Fi finally brought herself to ask Alexandria, who sat next to her. Up close, Fi could see how beautiful Alexandria was under the knight's armor. Her eyes were soft and reminded Fi of hickory wood. It was a beautiful contrast against the fire that colored her hair. If she did not choose the life of a knight, she would have had many men attempting to court her.

"It was something the chief told us when we returned. We are to take another elf from the village with us on our journey. Iam sees no problem in it as it provides further protection and assistance for us all. Erlan, on the other hand, is adamant we do not need her," she answered. "Personally, I do not care either way. I would like to get moving as staying here is wasting more time."

"Well, who is it the chief wants us to bring along with us?" Fi asked. She could not fathom why Erlan would not want one of his people to come along with them.

"We are to take Selain Willowood," Alexandria answered. The tone in her voice did not seem to indicate how she felt either way. She appeared to be more annoyed with the fact they were wasting more time fighting over a situation going to happen, regardless of how they all felt. Fi was confused on what the problem was with her joining with them.

"I wonder why Erlan would have such an issue with her coming along," Fi said aloud, almost to herself. She wondered if maybe they had a history that would cause him to not want her with them.

"Apparently, she is a little too excited about human life. Almost to the point she will put herself in compromising positions just to learn more about them. I think Erlan worries she could be a liability along the way and cause more issues than help," Alexandria answered as her head swung towards the door that had begun to open.

"As we enter human cities on our journey, what is to stop her from wandering off and causing problems? Problems we would have to solve. We do not have time to play babysitter to Selain while trying to achieve our objective. It is a burden I wish not to bear," Erlan said as he strode through the door. His chestnut hair flowed behind him with the movement. Fi could easily see the tension in his face. It was seeming to become the standard look for him lately as he'd lost his carefree and serene state.

"I don't know why you are fighting this so much. It appears

your father already made up his mind on the matter. Why get worked up over something that cannot be changed." Iam came in right behind him, eyes closed and hands behind his back. Whatever hostility that had been between the two of them was not lost. Iam opened his eyes, and the hazel had a tint of gold to them now. How much were his eyes able to change? All agitation faded, and he smiled under his goatee. As Erlan opened his mouth to continue his argument, Fi held up her hand to stop him.

"That's enough, Erlan. As big a risk as she may be during our travels, we are going to need all the help we can get if we want to succeed. In human settlements, we will be extra careful to keep your elvish lineage secret. We will have to work together to ensure she abides by that. I will not, however, turn down the aid of someone just because they are weak in one area. If that were the case, I would not be qualified for this journey in the least. So, stop your fighting. We need to get moving we have spent too much time here already."

The confidence in her voice sounded foreign. Was it not her just the other day who had tried to run and escape her problems? Maybe that is why now she knew it wouldn't solve anything. The only way to end the problem was to face him head-on. And to do that, they needed every ally they could muster. They could no longer stay in Pirn. They had to head to Adonia and see if they could find the refugee wizards. It was the only direction they currently had.

Chapter 11

The sky the next morning was a tender shade of pink that grew bolder as it neared the horizon. The closer it got, the more it appeared to melt into orange before finding the yellow sun peeking through the trees. A slight breeze shifted through the trees, causing their branches to wave, almost as if they were saying their goodbyes.

Chief Anrhil had seemed pleased that the group no longer protested the task of taking Selain with them. There appeared to be less strain in his face as they were packing. That tension passed on to Erlan. He said nothing all morning as he prepared his horse and supplies. The few times Fi tried to speak with him, he acted as though her voice was nothing but the wind.

This cold shoulder amused Selain every time she bore witness to it. A small grin would pull up the right side of her mouth. As it happened, she would turn away as to not let anyone see her take pleasure in Fi's failed attempts. Her humor was not lost to Fi, who had caught sight a couple of times. Fi knew there were bigger things to worry about than Selain.

"Everyone packed up?" Fi asked everyone as she tightened the saddlebag that sat on Hero's right hip. Everyone voiced they were ready, except Erlan, who had pulled his father over by a small cluster of trees. His face creased around his eyes. She turned away, not wanting to stare.

If Fi had to guess, he made one last attempt to persuade his father it was best if Selain were to remain in the village. What seemed mid-sentence, Anrhil turned away from his son, moving towards the group, leaving Erlan with his unfinished argument.

"I will pray that our ancestors watch over you in your travels. May they guide you in the direction that will lead you to success," he said to them before handing Fi a small pouch. Reaching inside, Fi pulled out a necklace of brown leather with a small glass vial, the size of a thimble. The vial was filled with an amethyst-colored liquid that sparkled as the sunlight shone through the glass. "This is the last of a great healing mixture from back when magic was still alive in our people. Every chief of this village has kept it safe and unknown to the rest of the elves."

"But…why give it to me? After all this time keeping it safe." Fi could not believe was she was holding. This was a piece of old magic. Pure untainted magic. She was not worthy to carry it around when her magic was tainted by its creation.

"There has been no greater time for this magic to have been needed. You, Fi Silvera, are the most important person in Abaddon. Should you find yourself in need of saving your life, drink this. If what has been passed down is true, it will heal any wound and cure any poison. Our world rests with all of you." He closed her hand over the small vial and gave her a reassuring smile.

Pressure fell on Fi. She trembled slightly as the truth of it all fully settled in. The fate of everyone was truly on her shoulders alone. While the group was there to assist her, in the end, it was she who had to end it all. She wasn't sure if it was possible, but she knew it was not something she could try to run from anymore. Her whole life she was hidden away for this. If she didn't succeed, everyone who died to keep her safe, like Alexandria's father, would have died in vain.

"Thank you, Anrhil. I hope we will meet again," Fi answered. This may be the last time that her eyes would see him or this village or even the woods that surrounded her home. The breeze rustled the leaves around her feet as her mind stopped drifting away and became sharp again.

With a swift movement, she pivoted away from the elvish chief and placed a foot into the stirrup of Hero's saddle. It gave good resistance as she put her body weight into it and swung her right leg over his body. The saddle felt warm from sitting against Hero's body. The feel of the leather so familiar was calming to her. She ran her hand over the familiar lines in the leather and the worn-in saddle horn from years of gripping.

"I will lead," Alexandria stated as she took the front spot on the road leading out of Pirn. "Iam, you will be behind me, then Fi, followed by Selain, and, Erlan, please, fall in as rear guard. With this order, there will be two riders in front of and behind Fi. This allows so that we can easily surround her for protection should the need arise. We will reconfigure once we come to a road wide enough for more than one horse."

No one objected to her idea as her reasoning was solid, and everyone fell into their place. Alexandria's pace was calm, as though they were simply taking a morning trail ride. They rode in silence as it would be quite difficult to speak to one another walking in a line. The trees were becoming thicker and wilder the further from Pirn they went. These woods seemed untouched besides the narrow trail they trekked on.

Animals could be heard rustling through the forest on either side of them. Their sounds indicated they were darting away from the trail and deeper into the trees. Being this far from a settlement, they were most likely not used to people being about. Besides the animals and the breeze through the trees, the only sounds were the horse's hooves hitting the trail.

They traveled for a week, ensuring when they stopped to make camp they could not be seen from the trail. It limited the use of fire for warmth, but they could not risk attention called to them by a passerby or, even worse, a Fiend. The trail had opened at times, allowing for Alexandria's original riding plan to be used. However, near the end of the week, the trail stayed narrow and did not seem to widen out again.

It wasn't until the sun had ascended higher into the sky, on the seventh day of travel, eliminating the pinks that revealed the clear blue sky above them did it change. Zephyr, Alexandria's horse, stopped in his tracks. His large brown eyes were wide and scanned the forest feverishly. The ring of gold around the luminous brown looked as though it wanted to escape. At once, Alexandria's right hand crossed to her left hip and grasped the hard hilt of her sword. She, too, looked around for an unknown attacker. Every muscle in her body on edge and ready to strike should the moment come.

The rest of the horses appeared to sense danger as well. Even Hero shifted nervously from one side to the other. Fi tried to see into the forest, but the canopy of the trees did not allow for a far sight of vision. Shadows appeared to be moving around them. She tried to determine if there was a source to the shadow or if fear was besting her. It was in that thought a large grayish-black blur appeared out of the darkness.

The first distinguishable feature was the creature's eyes. To

Fi, it looked as if two golden coins were slowly making their way towards her. They glistened and glowed, which gave off an eerie light. She sat on Hero, transfixed as the golden circles got closer and closer. Hero's body shuddered beneath her, seeming to recognize the source of the gold before she could.

More circles appeared behind the first. A crystal set of blue, pale and luminous, was to the left, and a pair of soft green, muted, almost absorbing the light, to the right. A twig made a snapping sound behind her, and she turned quickly, meeting a pair of dark brown steadfast eyes attached to what Fi could clearly see as a wolf. Behind it was another steely gray body surrounding them.

At once, Fi knew it was no average wolf. Its massive body stood easily two-and-a-half feet tall at the tops of its shoulders. Its paws were larger than they should have been, ending in twisted claws. The legs were long and lean and the fur on them was almost patchy. Her eyes traveled back to its face and its teeth were bared. As with the claws, they were twisted and did not seem to fit evenly together. This caused some teeth to stick out of the jaw at angles. The wolf's rich chocolate brown fur tousled in the light breeze that began rising around them. They must have been downwind and didn't even realize it.

Her eyes skimmed back to the three wolves on her left that had now come into view. She could see a tawny smaller wolf on the left and a reddish-brown wolf on the right. The golden eyes belonged to a large, almost jet-black wolf. Where there wasn't black it appeared, gray had begun to set in. Her eyes stayed on the black wolf. His demeanor, and the way the other wolves responded, gave the appearance he was the pack lead.

Something didn't seem right about the wolves around them, besides their strange physical features. Fi had dealt with wolves on many occasions while living on the farm. They would attempt to attack the livestock in the night, and then she and Byron would go and hunt down the invaders. She had never known wolves to attack a group of travelers in this manner.

Wolves had never taken this long to attack an enemy or potential prey in the past. Everything wolves do is almost choreographed. A hunt was almost a dance in which each wolf had its role to play. Why were these wolves still sitting and waiting? What was it they were after? Out of nowhere, the wolves made their attack.

The ring of Alexandria's sword echoed throughout the entirety of the woods. She skillfully maneuvered Zephyr as the tawny wolf made its launch. If Alexandria had been two seconds slower, the wolf would have gotten the legs of her horse. She brought down her sword in an attempt to behead the wolf as it landed, but it dodged at the last moment.

The path was still too narrow to close in around Fi as intended, so they were to fight as they stood. These were not ideal conditions, and the wolf's patterns made it worse. Instead of going for the neck of Selain's horse, Verca, the small gray wolf went for Selain's left leg, creating a large gash with its teeth. She let out an echoing scream as her leather traveling pants became stained red.

"Selain!" Fi could hear Erlan cry out helplessly from behind. A sound of worry and desperation in his voice. While he was close to her, he had a wolf of his own holding his attention. The reddish-brown wolf had launched itself at Erlan before he could get the arrow loose. When he fired, the arrow went just below, hitting where the wolf had been standing. He was barely able to move out of the way fast enough as the wolf missed landing on the other side of him.

Fi was so desperate, looking around to see how everyone was faring she forgot there were five wolves attacking them. She took her eyes off Iam, who was now off Ithil, battling on the ground with the large brown wolf. She had seen blood on his body but did not know to whom the blood belonged. As she turned her head, her eyes locked with the black-bodied wolf.

It snapped its jaw at her while slowly taking steps closer to her and Hero. She could hear the low, chilling growl escaping its throat. She slowly reached for her bow, but with every movement, the wolf's growl grew louder. Almost as if it knew what she was doing. She needed to decide and do it fast. In a swift motion, she grabbed her bow and went to notch an arrow. At the movement, however, the wolf made its move.

Hero tried to move his body out of the way, but the wolf was just a little faster. It leaped from its perch on a nearby rock and took Fi clear off Hero's back. She hit the ground hard on her left shoulder, sending pain radiating down her entire arm. Instantaneously, she knew it had come out of its socket. Her head felt dizzy from the landing and the pain. She shook it, trying to clear away the fog. Pressure mounted in her chest, almost as though she was being smothered. She opened her eyes to the black wolf with one paw on her chest, the other by her head. It was going for the death bite.

She couldn't fight it. She couldn't even move her arm, no matter how much she tried to. She looked into the eyes of her killer. The gold held no fascination to her now. It had lost its luster and looked dull and cheap. Its breath was hot and strong on her face as it lowered down. She closed her eyes, waiting for the pain of the wolf ripping out her neck.

"Fi! No!" In the distance, she heard Iam calling out as he had undoubtedly been able to see her and the black wolf. A whine of a wolf came a moment later, and the breath on her neck intensified. Her heart felt as though it was going to beat out of her chest as time slowed down and tortured her in her last moments.

The weight released from her chest as a growl escaped the wolf. Iam had struck the black wolf's shoulder first off Fi. He was covered in blood and standing over her defensively, breathing hard. The wolf turned back towards them, still growling and baring its fangs. More whines of wolves could be heard around them as other members made contact.

With a howl, the black wolf ran at Iam. Any sign of intelligence had left its eyes and was replaced by a feral need to kill. Iam stood with his short swords up, ready to take on the assailant when an arrow came from the path and hit it square in the heart, dropping it mid-stride. It came to a stop at Iam's feet where, with the danger passed, he dropped, too.

"Fi! Fi, please, tell me you are okay?" He quickly turned to her, looking her up and down. Tears welled in her eyes as her adrenaline subsided. He picked her up into his arms, and she winced. "What is it?" he asked as he gently laid her back down. By this time, she could hear everyone assessing the damages made by the wolves.

"My...shoulder. I think it is dislocated," Fi said through gritted teeth. With the adrenaline subsiding, the pain intensified. She knew how to reset one but not on herself. Pushing herself into a seated position with her right arm, she laid the left in her lap. Scattered along the path were the remains of all five wolves.

Erlan helped Selain off Verca to better assess the bite to her leg. He laid her on the ground and tore open the bottom of her pants. Four angry bleeding lines were clear to see, even from Fi's distance. Erlan quickly took some of the fabric of her pants and pressed into the wound. Selain grit her teeth and threw her head back as a new round of pain came over her. Erlan's eyes reflected the pain she was enduring.

Alexandria made her way around the wolves, ensuring they were all indeed dead. Her sword dripped with fresh blood, creating a small trail behind her as she walked. As she approached each wolf, she quickly thrust her sword through its skull. Each blow made a sickening crunch as the bone split.

"Iam, do you know how to reset a shoulder?" Fi brought her eyes back to meet Iam's. She could see now, like Selain, he had four claw marks running down the right side of his neck. They were nowhere near as deep as Selain's, but blood still slowly wept out. "Iam, your neck!" She fought hard to sit up more and use her good arm to put pressure on it.

"It's nothing. I'm fine. I barely even feel anything." He lifted his hand, wiping some of the blood off the wound. He stared at it, almost not believing it came from his own body. "Huh..." With that, he fell to the ground in a large heap.

"Erlan! Alexandria! Help!" Fi called out loudly, trying to get anyone's attention. She successfully got all eyes on her. Erlan was still assisting Selain, so Alexandria ran over with haste. She bent down and felt along Iam's neck for a pulse. It didn't take her long to be able to find it. She slowly rolled him onto his side and placed pressure on the claw marks. She looked around for a piece of cloth, yet found none.

"Fi, I need you to put gentle pressure on his neck so I can get something from my pack." Fi stared at her, almost not hearing her words. "Fi, listen to me, please."

"I-I can't move. My shoulder is dislocated." Her response was weak and felt almost as if she were making an excuse. Before she could form another thought, Alexandria whipped around and had a hold on Fi's injured arm. And then, *pop*, quick relief and a new sense of pain. Everything was still raw, and the muscles around her shoulder and begun to swell and tighten.

"There. Now, use your good arm and put pressure on the damn wound." The bite in Alexandria's voice was enough to pull Fi from her pain. She slowly got to her knees and placed her right hand over the wound. The blood was thick and warm against her clammy hands. She still had tears spilling from her eyes and it made small streaks and trails through the blood and dirt on the back of her hands. She felt she sat there for an eternity before Alexandria returned.

She moved Fi's hand off Iam's neck without saying a word. In her hand was a small tin container that had a small latch. As she opened it, Fi could see it contained a greenish-colored salve. Alexandria scooped some out with her fingers and spread it across Iam's wound. After a few minutes, the salve solidified, and the bleeding stopped.

"That should hold him until we get to the next town. Hopefully, they know someone there with has some medical skills."

"How long is that going to be?" Fi looked at Iam's lifeless body and knew he needed proper medical help as soon as possible.

"We should be at a town by afternoon. I wasn't planning on stopping there but, now, we have no choice." She stood up and walked over to Zephyr, removing his saddle and tying it on top of Iam's horse for safekeeping. Upon returning, she picked up Iam with some effort.

"Erlan, can you help me a moment?" she called over her shoulder as she made her way back to Zephyr. With Erlan's help, Alexandria was able to mount her horse while Iam laid across Zephyr's back in front of her. It wasn't an ideal way to travel, but they had no other choice. With Ithil tied behind Erlan, they made their way to the next town, praying they did not run into anything else the rest of the day.

Chapter 12

That morning seemed bent on lengthening. Fi felt as though the sun had purposely slowed its ascent, further cursing their journey. The feeling of helplessness weighed heavily on her as she watched Iam's head bob lifelessly over Zephyr's back. His hair had come out of its leather band during the fight and fell across his face. The ointment Alexandria had placed on his neck appeared to hold the wound together, though they had to stop twice to reapply it. Fi feared they didn't have long until that would no longer work as an option.

Guilt filled her at the thought of his wounds reopening and his death being her fault. Did they happen because he became distracted by her plight? Was saving her life going to cost him his? She had not known him more than a few days, but her heart pulled at the thought of losing him. He had chosen to come along on the journey with them. He was not pulled in by a bound duty. Why had he done so?

The reality of the whole situation she was in hit her, and she felt sickened. She was the one the elves said was prophesied to end it, so the others would be putting their lives before hers. Fi knew this when leaving Pirn, but the reality of it all sank in. To her, their lives were just as important as hers, yet she knew in truth. That was not the case.

They continued down the worn dirt path until it opened up to a wider road. It was no longer deep-packed reddish dirt but laid cobblestone. They appeared to fit together like a badly formed puzzle. The road here at the end was in rough shape. It did not appear to be traveled often, so the upkeep was kept to a minimum. The grout holding the deep gray cobblestones together was loose, causing them to fall away from one another. Rain had seized this opportunity and caused greater erosion.

Areas of the road were being reclaimed by the forest. Tree roots and vines growing through the cracks. The horses carefully made their way over jutting stones and roots that attempted to trip them. This created a slowed pace until the road came to a more cared for section. The further they rode, the smoother and sturdier the road became. The grout became firm, and the pieces fit together beautifully.

There was no brush covering the stones as there was when first coming across it. They walked two horses side by side as originally planned, with some changes. Alexandria and Selain took the front while Erlan walked with Ithil. This left Fi in the middle alone, which is how she felt right now.

As the sun was making its way past midday, they came over a crest of a hill, and Fi could see a town below. Like its streets, the buildings were made of cobblestones pieced together. The closer they got, the more detail Fi could see in the buildings. The houses and buildings had been carefully crafted and pieced together. Each had two stories, and the windows had clear glass instead of shutters to keep out the cold. Many of the buildings looked identical to the one standing beside it. There was little to differentiate one building from the next.

Intense planning must have taken place as the city was built.

Each building was almost skillfully lined up with the one next to it. This created perfectly straight streets throughout the city. The strategic arrangement allowed many buildings while still allowing for space. It made Baydell look as though it was thrown together overnight.

When originally built, the buildings must have been beautiful. Now, the houses were covered in thick green moss. It was as though the forest attempted to reclaim the city. Ivy had begun climbing some of the buildings, weaving itself into the moss. It made the city appear wild and primitive, even with the detailed stonework.

Upon entering the city, Erlan and Selain pulled hoods over their heads to conceal their elf ears. While Baydell was accepting of the elves, they were the minority. It was best to try to keep their lineage a secret as long as they could. They did so just in time as people emerged from their homes to begin their day.

It didn't take long for the people to notice travelers coming from the western road. Many of the townsfolk stop to look at the strange sight. It wasn't until one caught sight of Iam's body that they took heed.

"Call for a healer. One of them is injured!" a gruff voice came from the crowd. This was followed by two children running into town quickly. The crowd parted, ensuring they were able to move into town without resistance. As they went through the crowd, they were met with uneasy eyes. They may have been willing to help the injured, but it appeared that their trust was not easily gained.

The horses traveled through town past what Fi assumed was their marketplace, shops could be seen as the horses took them deeper into the city. Though none seemed open, the owners could be seen peeking out their front doors to catch a sight at the outsiders in town. Fi could not determine if the welcome they were getting was friendly or contingent.

Coming to the end of the long road was what Fi thought was their city square. A large open area sat with grassy patches along its edges. Carts had been moved to allow for more space. Though some of their proprietors did not seem happy with having to move from what was most likely a prime spot. Glancing around them, a man caught Fi's eye. He looked to be in his late forties and on the heavier side. He stroked his tawny brown beard, and when Fi met his brown eyes, she felt a chill run down her spine. She hastened to look anywhere but back at him.

An older woman in a long white dress came running into the square from in front of them. Her ginger hair with trails of gray running through it flowed behind her. In her hand was a large bag that looked as though it would have been heavy to carry. She stopped in front of them, catching her breath, and her pale blue eyes landed on Iam.

"Please, bring him this way," she said in an assertive voice. "My clinic is over here, and I need to look at his wounds at once." She led them to a cobblestone building to their right. Although it looked identical to its neighbor, it bore a sign over the door containing a red mortar and pestle.

Alexandria and Erlan carefully removed Iam's body from Zephyr. Erlan worked carefully to ensure his hood stayed up. They carried him inside and laid him on a clean bed and moved out of the way. The clinic was of decent size. Three more beds were against the same wall as Iam's. Near the back was a stone counter that had different herbs and medicines stored. Fi recognized a few of them, but many were new to her. Bottles of bright-colored liquids reflected the little light that reached that far back into the clinic.

The walls reflected their cobblestone counterparts on the exterior. The stone floor was free of any dirt except what they had just brought in. The shop as a whole appeared to be kept meticulously clean. Fi wondered how it was done so well. The small herbalist in Baydell always complained about customers making it impossible to have anything sterile.

Fi could only stand back by everyone else and hope he would be okay. The woman quickly assessed him. His shirt was pulled back to determine the severity of his wounds. The healer's breath caught as her eyes fell on the damage he had taken. To Fi, this did not seem like a good sign for his recovery. A necklace fell off his left shoulder as she gently rolled his body to work. It was a simple braided brown leather cord that held some kind of shiny metal in the shape of a shield. No ornate carvings lay in it that she could see.

The woman removed the salve Alexandria had been placing on the wound to stop the bleeding. Quickly, she realized the wound was not going to close on its own. She applied pressure while pulling out what looked like a needle and thread. She masterfully began sewing the sides of the wound together. Iam was still unconscious and did not even so much as grimace when the needle pierced his skin. With every stitch, the lacerations bled less and less. She was able to close what his body could not.

Upon completion of the needlework, she stood and retrieved a bowl and towel from a cupboard. Filling the bowl from a pitcher, she made her way back to Iam to finish cleaning the blood that remained on his body. After thirty minutes, it seemed as though the woman was satisfied with her work.

"He is not out of the woods yet. If he survives until tomorrow, I say his chances are great," she explained, placing the bowl on the table near his bedside. Relief flushed over Fi.

"Thank you. Thank you so much," Fi said. Her voice shook as the emotions from the journey mixed with the relief she felt. The woman walked over and placed her hand on Fi's shoulder. Both Erlan and Alexandria took a step closer as a protective reaction. If the woman took notice, she did not move away.

"How do we pay you for your services, miss…?" Alexandria spoke in a consistent, calm voice. She gave off no aura of mistrust. How could she after everything the woman had just done? It was apparent. However, her guard would not be put down, even for a healer.

"My name is Ninnete Linyeve, but you can just call me Nin. As for payment, we can discuss that at a later time. You all look as though you could use a little care as well. Maybe even some food and proper sleep." Nin smiled warmly at them as she spoke. Genuine care and concern could be felt emanating from her.

"I-I don't want Iam to be alone," Fi replied in a small voice. She knew he wouldn't know the difference, but the thought of him lying in the bed in a strange town upset her.

"I will stay with him," Erlan spoke softly to her right. There was a pain in his voice as he spoke, as though his brain spoke words his heart did not mean. "He saved your life, so I will sit with him in gratitude. I only ask you bring me back some food with you." His face did not shift towards hers as he spoke but fell to the floor. As Fi placed her hand on his arm in thanks, his body stiffened slightly.

"Thank you, Erlan," was all she could muster as a response. Removing her arm, she turned to Nin to have her begin patching up the rest of them. Many of their wounds superficial and easy to clean and mend. The exception being Selain's leg. Nin used the same stitching technique she utilized earlier to fully close the bite wounds down her leg.

Once Fi's scrapes and scratches were cleaned, she made her way to Iam's side. It was difficult to look at him in his current state. His usual cocky smile was not plastered across his face. It was eerie to see a man who could never sit still so tranquil. Much of the color in his skin was missing, leaving a pale, blanched tone. Fi wondered if it was from losing so much blood. If it wasn't for his even breathing, he may have been mistaken for dead.

"I'll be back, okay? When I come back, you better still be breathing. You will not die because of me, you understand?" The last line she whispered, trying to keep her guilt to herself. She, of course, knew the elves would hear her same as if she shouted it. She clutched his hand as she spoke, noticing it felt oddly cooler than the last time she had held it. Standing, she joined Alexandria and Selain by the door. Together, the three women walked into town, leaving both Iam and Erlan behind.

By the time the ladies went back into town, the daily activities were in full swing. People of the city traversed up and down the street to go in and out of the now open shops. Their attire was much different than Fi was used to back in Baydell. Back home, it was not uncommon for the citizens to wear their farming clothes while they shopped. Really, the only time one would see anything that didn't have some kind of dirt on them was if they attended a temple gathering or a festival such as the one they just had taken place.

Though, here in Windcall, no one looked dirty or as though they had ever worked on a farm. Many of the women wore dresses of fine material ranging in colors of reds, greens, and blues. The sleeves fell delicately at their elbows. Some having excess material continuing to flow from them, creating a cascading, billowing trail in the air. Almost all were tightly fitted to the body, Fi guessed to accentuate their feminine figures. Hem lines ended just above the ankle, allowing them to stay dry if rain were to create pools along the roads.

The women's hair was intricately braided and tied back as no strand escaped the work that was done. Little girls held their mother's hand in simple dresses that matched the color of their mother's. The state of their hair was less complex and simple pigtail braids were done with a matching bow on each one.

The men were more casual than the women. They wore clean trousers in shades of brown and black. Their cotton shirts more subdued and earth-toned. The only appearance that resembled Baydell was that of the young boys. They wore clothing that had seen better days and were covered in dirt from play.

"Should we look for food?" Alexandria's voice asked to Fi's left. Fi nodded in response and started walking towards the shops they passed coming into town. Though she knew she should eat, at present, she was not hungry. Having witnessed the stitching of Iam, she felt more nauseous than hungry. Still, she continued because who knew when the next time they would have this opportunity again.

Walking through town quickly became uncomfortable. As they passed the citizens, their gaze always fell to them. It was as though they were intruders in a city and needed to be watched carefully. Even the children stared at them in curiosity. They then decided instead of going to what was most likely a wonderful tavern full of patrons to find something smaller. A tavern with very little traffic to attempt to have a little peace.

After some debate on where to eat, they settled on a tavern called The Future Lily. The wooden sign out front depicted a snow-white lily beneath its name written in the same color. Tables were strewn inside without consideration of spacing. Some tables nearly touched, while others had a two-foot gap between them. Tables and chairs were old, and many had nicks taken out of them.

The walls had mounted animal heads with a layer of dust clearly seen from the tables. There was a bar against the back wall, if one could call it that. It was a couple of planks of old wood nailed to thick boards forming legs. Fi would not trust it to hold a single drink, let alone a drink and meal for the six stools that were at it.

Of all the places they observed, it seemed the least crowded. It was clear why it was not busy. Fi wondered about how the quality of food may have been so much better at a nicer tavern. However, with them being watched and Selain needing to keep her race a secret, this was the best option. They were able to procure a table in a far corner, giving them more privacy and Alexandria a full view of the tavern.

The menu choices were limited to roasted meat, cheese, bread, and a few savory pies. Alexandria and Selain had no issues enjoying their meal. Fi just could not get a single bite to look appetizing. She poked at her meat with a fork as Selain spoke to her.

"You are going to have to pierce it harder than that if you want to actually get it to your mouth," Selain commented through her tone it was not made out of concern. Fi raised her head with a blank look on her face.

"Huh?" she had not heard what Selain had said but registered she was being talked to. Her mind was so full it was easier just to push everything away. "I'm sorry, did you say something?"

"You have been sitting there playing with your food for the last ten minutes," Selain answered her back now with a curious look on her face. "You're not still thinking about what's his name, are you?"

"Iam. What's his face's name is Iam. And, yeah, sorry for caring about the welfare of someone who risked his life for mine," Fi shot back before controlling her tongue. Selain knew full well Iam's name, and Fi fell right into her trap to get her angry. Though she did not know why this was the goal.

"Shh. Keep your voices down. The last thing we need is attention drawn to us," Alexandria said through gritted teeth. The look in her hickory eyes could be compared to a mother scolding her children discreetly in public. The threat of a good beating when they returned home. Both Fi and Selain recoiled slightly but lowered their voices.

"Right, him. Look, there is a good chance he will be fine, and you guys can continue this weird romance you have going on." Fi's face went red and hot at Selain's assumption. There was no relationship at all. She barely knew him truthfully.

"There is no romance! I met him the day before I came to Pirn. I... There..." Fi began, but she didn't know where to go with it. Selain read the situation completely wrong.

"No man meets a girl, follows to her house only to hear she is to leave, and then follows her again risking his neck over and over if he doesn't feel something for her," Selain continued with her reasonings, "Think about it, everyone in Baydell knows the punishment for entering Pirn without invitation yet he did it, anyway. And he threw himself in front of a big, mutated wolf in an attempt to save you. Granted, in the end, it was Erlan who killed it, but the action stands. Something is definitely between you two."

Fi's heart squeezed. Everything she said could be taken in that context. Though he barely knew her, he risked life and limb to follow and kept her safe. Love at first sight doesn't exist except in fairytales. All of it had to be a simple misunderstanding of the situation. Simple.

"Or maybe you haven't noticed because of another reason." Fi's eyes went back to Selain's face as she spoke again. Her face this time had grown hard and lost the lightness it had before. "Maybe you haven't noticed Iam's feelings for you because you have been too encased in your feelings for someone else." At that moment, Fi's entire body turned to ice. Any heat that resided from her embarrassment earlier was completely gone. She could almost feel the color draining from her face.

"Fi Silvera, relationships of that romantic nature are forbidden!" Alexandria quickly caught on to what was being implied between the two women in front of her. This made the situation so much worse. Selain had called her out, and Alexandria drove home why her feelings were not allowed to be there. She had to try and fix this.

"No, no, it's nothing like that at all. Erlan is a dear friend to me and has been since I can remember. If anything, he is like an older brother to me not a lover," she waved her hands in front of her face to drive home the point. Her heart ached with the lie, but she knew it had to be that way. "I am just completely dense and didn't realize Iam may feel more for me than a simple friendship. Though I don't know my feelings about him as of now, who knows, right?"

A completely weak argument, but it was all she could think of. Alexandria appeared to buy what she said, but Selain gave her a look if understanding and it wasn't the lie, she understood. What in the world did she have going on inside her head? Letting the matter go for the moment, she turned her body towards Alexandria.

"What about you, 'Drea? Any love prospects for you?" Selain asked slyly. Alexandria almost choked on the ale she was taking a drink of. Her eyes wide, a slight pink appearing beneath her freckles.

"No, not for me at the moment. Haven't had time to think about that with knight training and now the mission at hand," she said quickly still while clearing her throat of the inhaled ale. "Maybe someday, I will consider it but, as of right now, it is the furthest thing from my mind. Priorities. Also, do not call me 'Drea. It's Alexandria." This was the first time Fi had seen Alexandria flustered.

"Okay, 'DREA, we survive this, and I'll help you to get a good husband." Selain threw her head back, laughing and, as she did, her hood slipped down her head, revealing her ears to the few patrons and the bartender in the tavern.

Chapter 13

Selain's eyes widened as she felt the air tickle her now exposed ears. Silverware and tankards could be heard dropping around the bar. The tankards shattered on impact with the stone floor. Slowly, Fi and Selain turned to look at the other patrons that Alexandria had already locked eyes with. Their faces did not show acceptance as they did in Baydell but portrayed anger and fear.

"What gives you the right to think you can come into our town, Fairy?" a man's voice came from the bar. Selain instantly turned red at the biggest insult one could call an elf. In ancient lore, fairies were small and vile creatures. They caused nothing but trouble and destruction wherever they went. Humans finally ended their destructive ways by wiping out the race completely. The same way almost all humans feel now about the elves.

The man turned towards them, and Fi saw it was the cart owner she saw that morning. If she felt uncomfortable with his eyes on them before, it was nothing compared to now. Selain's fists were turning white as she clenched them, trying to control herself. But it was Alexandria who stood and spoke out.

"And you know well that King Pierce, in his time, had granted pardon to the elves in his kingdom. There is no law that prevents them from entering any city here," her voice rang clear as her hand rested on the hilt of her sword. A fire burned behind her eyes, which caused even Fi to flinch. The man took a step back before answering her.

"I believe that the old king was soft in his acceptance of the traitors. What is to stop the few that remained from repeating the acts of the past? Fairies can never be trusted," he finished, staring straight at Selain, burning the insult further into her heart.

With that, a *ring* filled that tavern as a movement crossed Fi's vision. Within moments, Alexandria had bounded over the table and had her sword to the man's neck. The redness brought on by anger no longer filled his face. Every ounce of color had fallen away. His deep brown eyes were wide as he stared into the woman holding his life in her hands.

"I dare you to insult my companion one more time." The words were hard through gritted teeth. Her breathing labored as she attempted to keep herself somewhat composed. No one in the tavern moved to his aid. They all were frozen at the scene that had unfolded in front of him.

"A-ight, Lance, you've caused me enough problems today. I think it's time for you to get back to your cart." A squat old man came sauntering out a door that Fi had not realized was there. He appeared to be in his late fifties, with a head full of chalk-white hair. It stuck up in every which way and was beginning to thin. The hair migrated over his neck and arms, which was a strong contrast to his sepia skin.

Alexandria slowly released Lance from her grip, not taking her eyes off him. Her jaw stayed clenched as he quickly sidled past her and went out the door. It wasn't until she was sure he was not going to return did she sheath her sword.

"Sorry for the trouble, sir. I am not normally one to lose my temper in such a way. I understand if you with us to leave as well," Alexandria said as she turned on her heels to the old man.

"I ain't kicking you out. He was the one who started the commotion. Just finish your food and leave before a riot breaks out in the tavern." He threw a hand into the air as he returned to the room he was in behind the hidden door. All eyes were on them as Alexandria made her way back to the table.

"Let's take the food we have and leave. Erlan is most likely starving at this point." In agreement, the three of them packed up as much of the food on the table as they could carry. Before leaving, Selain lifted the hood back over her ears. Though, at this point, word may have spread about the true nature of who she was.

The walk back carried an air that Fi's thought was correct. Though many had watched them before, more out of probable curiosity then threat, their faces now showed animosity and fear. Children's faces were uneasy, and they would hide behind their parents. If Iam's condition were not as dire as it was, they made to leave Windcall at once.

"I did not realize the hatred we had in human cities." Selain said quietly. "I've ever really known the acceptance of Baydell. It explains why the chief forbid me from venturing to other human cities."

"I wish I could say this town was an outlier. But in truth it is commonplace for the racism to run rampant. It is important you do not wander off and try to explore as we travel further." Alexandria said. She placed a reassuring hand on Selain's shoulder.

"I understand," was all Selain could muster.

The closer they got to the clinic, the faster their pace became. A crowd gathered outside the clinic. Many of the men concentrated around the entrance and talked loudly amongst themselves.

"Lance said the female with the hood was really a dirty fairy!"

"The one's in there came in with her!"

With Alexandria leading, they pushed their way through the crowd. Selain between her and Fi to keep her from the crowd. The men realized who they were quickly and began shouting at them. So many things said hurt even Fi, and they were not directed towards her. Anger built in her stomach. She could almost taste acid in her mouth as it formed.

Fi was overcome by a cold sweat as her body's temperature rose out of control. She knew what was coming. It was the same feeling she had before setting the fire at the festival. The sensations mimicked when she stood against Anrhil to save Iam's life. Fi knew she had to get control before things went from bad to catastrophic.

"Everyone, go home!" a woman's voice rang out over the crowd. "I have a patient in here trying to rest, and that isn't going to happen with everyone out here shouting." It was Nin who had emerged from the clinic, apparently annoyed with the ruckus. Her eyes were filled with not anger but disappointment in the behavior of the townsfolk.

"We ain't leaving, Nin," a voice said from the crowd. "I know I for one do not feel safe knowing one of them is here. No, I am here to ensure they leave promptly. The voice belonged to none other than Lance. His words rallied the crowd back into a frenzy. Such blind hatred not far from Baydell, which was welcoming and understanding of the elves.

"I wasn't asking, Lance," Nin shot back at him coldly. "Those who choose to stay and further disrupt my patient's recovery will no longer have access to my aid. I will cut off all medicine and will dress no wounds." At this, the crowd went silent. The men looked back and forth with one another, almost communicating without speaking. After a few minutes, the crowd quickly disbursed, leaving Lance alone in front of the shop.

"I'm not happy about what side you are taking, Nin, but I would be a fool to risk losing your aid. Just watch your back," he said in defeat. He glanced over at Selain with his last words. Turning on his heels, he turned around and sulked away from the clinic.

All four women went inside. Erlan sat defensively in front of Iam unsure of who it was that would be entering through the door. When his eyes caught who it was, he relaxed, and the dagger in his right hand lowered. Iam was still unconscious on the bed but had regained much of his color. Fi was relieved to see he was doing well, but her mind wandered to what Selain had said about how he felt.

She felt her heart quicken at the thought of it. How had it not crossed her mind? Looking at the situation as a whole it made sense how Selain had seen it. It just didn't make sense. She had met him briefly before her mark manifested to the point she needed to leave. There was no way in that short period he could have developed anything for her.

Yet, here he was, joining them on a dangerous journey for no other reason than her. He risked death, twice, for her. Was she so focused on what lay ahead that she shut it out? No, that wasn't the reason. Her eyes moved to Erlan as he talked in elvish to Selain. That was the reason she didn't notice.

Her heart belonged to someone who could not take it. Selain reminded her today how true that was. Making her way to Iam, she took his hand in hers. The warmth that had been distant bloomed in it now.

"Thank you for helping us, Nin. I hope it will not cause trouble for you in the future," Fi said, turning her head towards Nin, who mixed two liquids behind the counter.

"Do not worry about it," she answered without even raising her eyes. "I am the only healer in the city. For them to cause me any problems would be their undoing, and they know it. For now, you all need rest. Please, stay here as long as you need."

With safety now secured, fatigue set into Fi. The events of travel and the wolves wore out any adrenaline she had remaining. Her full stomach lent to the idea of a nap. She could not bring herself to remove her hand from Iam's. She could not explain it, but she did not want to go too far from him. It had to be the guilt she felt for his current situation. She opted to sit next to his bed and lie her head on it. She could hear Alexandria talking about how she did not need rest and would be staying awake. Sleep then quickly overtook Fi's mind.

When she stirred awake, Fi felt pressure on her hand. Slowly, she lifted her head and saw Iam's bright hazel eyes staring back at her. She jumped back, almost pulling him out of the bed. Her cheeks burning that she had held his hand the entire time.

"Ouch! Hey, careful! I'm still hurt, you know," Iam said to her, smiling through the pain. The cocky smirk returned to his face, and Fi felt her heart quickening. She tried to remove her hand from his, but he would not release it. Glancing around, Fi saw everyone else was asleep, including Alexandria. Nin was nowhere to be seen. Darkness grew outside, and she must have slept the entire rest of the day. It was only her and Iam that were awake.

"Iam, you can let go of my hand now," Fi said quietly. The last thing she wanted was to wake anyone and have them find her in a precarious situation. Once again, she tried to free her hand, but he held firm. She looked at Iam's face, trying to understand why he would not let go.

"I think I will hold it just a little longer," his voice had dropped and, while still playful, it was not as light as it usually was. An intensity burned behind his eyes, and Fi's gaze trailed over to the sewn skin on his shoulder.

"I don't understand you, Iam," she said without thinking. He blinked at her, not understanding what she had meant. There was no way Selain was right, but Fi had to know. "I don't understand how you and me meeting randomly at the festival compelled you to follow me…us. You have put yourself in harm's way for me twice, almost dying for me." Her eyes glanced again to the wound. "Why? Why do all this when you could have gone about your life?" It all came spilling out, though she didn't ask the one question burning in her mind.

Iam sat silent for a second. He appeared taken off guard by her line of questioning. As though he had never stopped to think about it himself. His brows creased, and his hand squeezed hers.

"I-I honestly don't know. Remember when I told you in Pirn how I couldn't explain why I followed you. That feeling overcame me again when that wolf stood over you. I didn't even think I just reacted. At that point, it didn't matter what happened to me, as long as you were protected." Iam released her hand and ran it through his hair. Fi did not move her hands away as she had previously been trying to do. "I know it sounds crazy, and it probably is, but the thought of something happening to you..." His voice cut off.

Selain was right. She was right about everything. Fi had ignored the obvious signs of Iam's feelings. Everything he had done was not for the sake of the prophecy, but for her alone. She didn't know how to react to his answer. Fi could feel every beat of her heart in her chest. She was surprised that Iam could not hear it as she did in her ears.

In her whole life, no one professed feelings to her. Sure, she was courted a few times, but it never led to anything. And the one she wanted it most from would never return her feelings. Yet, here was a guy that is willing to throw himself in front of a wolf for her. What was she supposed to do? What was she supposed to say?

"You don't have to say anything. I know I probably sound like a madman. But something tells me you are important and must be protected. I can't explain it.," Iam said as he slid his hand back into her, interlacing their fingers. "I don't want you to say anything because I told you how I felt. Or because I threw a wolf off you. I know how I felt came out of left field. A week or so ago you and I never spoke. But you asked the question why. I am not going to lie to you. He squeezed her hand again, and her heart skipped a beat.

"You are right. I have only really met you. And with everything happening, a relationship is low on my priorities. But, please, be more careful with yourself. Don't make my decision for me, understand?" she answered. No matter how he felt about her, it was not worth his life.

"I make no promises. You tend to like to throw yourself into dangerous situations by habit," he said, chuckling to himself, which made him wince.

"You need to get more rest. Now, close your eyes and get some sleep," she told him. Fi made her way to get up and move to a bed. He was obviously going to be okay, and she worried for nothing. She met resistance as Iam curled his fingers around hers. She turned back to look at him, and he had his cocky smile on his face.

"Can you leave your hand here with me?" He tried to be as serious as he could through a chuckle. Fi rolled her eyes, smiling as she finally pulled her hand free of Iam's.

"Good night, Iam," she said as she crawled into the only empty bed left staring at the hand now becoming cool, losing the heat of his. Her face felt warm, and she knew in light anyone would see her blushed cheeks. It was hard to believe what had really just happened. Now, she had to figure out how she felt.

As she was getting comfortable, she heard a throat clear behind her. She quickly turned over and saw Erlan staring back at her. Her cheeks, which had felt warm before, now blazed. How long had he been awake? Even if he hadn't been awake long, he had to have heard Iam's confession to her. His eyes stood out in the darkness. Pain was etched into his eyes, as though they were truly crystal that had cracked.

Fi's heart lost all excitement and barely beat in her chest. The elation from Iam's words was replaced with guilt. There was no reason to feel guilty, but here she was looking at Erlan, feeling as though she had done something wrong. She opened her mouth to say something but could not think of what to say. Upon closing her mouth again, Erlan swiftly rolled away from her.

The clinic was dead silent except for the sounds of deep

breathing. In a matter of moments, her heart swelled and deflated to the point of pain. Fi curled into a ball in her bed, confused about how she should feel. She longed for the days that all she dreaded were the chores on the farm. Not worrying about prophecies and matters of the heart. Her last thoughts were of Byron and how all she wanted now was to talk with him and find out what she should do.

Chapter 14

As tired as Fi had been lying on her bed, she fought to sleep all night. Her body was exhausted from travel and battle. Yet her mind would not quiet. Many thoughts at once crowded and fought for attention. If it wasn't the prophecy, it was Iam, Erlan, and what the future would hold. It was more than one mind should have been able to hold.

As the sun shined through the windows of the clinic, Fi conceded and slowly sat up in her bed. The braid in which she wore disheveled from a night of tossing and turning. Alexandria appeared to have been awake for quite some time already. She stood near the back of the clinic as Selain asked Nin a new question every moment.

"What does this herb do? And this one cures what ailment? Would it be a bad idea to mix these two?" Where most people would be annoyed at the millions of questions, Nin took it in stride, seeming to enjoy passing on the knowledge to an eager student.

Iam was still asleep in his bed, but Erlan was nowhere to be seen. Like Alexandria's and Selain's, his bed was perfectly made. The white sheets were crisply folded and appeared as though no one had slept in them the night before.

"Ah, you're awake. We were wondering how long you were going to sleep." Nin's voice rose over Selain's questions. "I wasn't sure what time you moved to an actual bed last night to get some quality sleep." Fi held back a scoff at her last statement. Her sleep last night was anything but quality. Unfortunately, the heaviness of her face must have been obvious.

"You probably should have moved sooner. You look dead on your feet and the day has just started," Selain said. "You sure you don't need to lie back down?" Fi couldn't tell if Selain was being genuine in her remarks. Fatigue had a way of interfering with perception and decision-making.

"No, I'm good. I am just slow to wake up in the morning. You could ask my cousin..." No, not her cousin, her sister. Fi caught her thoughts and tried to continue quickly. "Mariah would tell you how fed up she was with me being late to morning chores. Never got the hang of being a morning person is all. By the way, where is Erlan?" She hoped her tired demeanor would hide the pain that pulled on her heart. Selain and Alexandria exchanged looks with one another.

"We are not entirely sure. I was the first to wake this morning and his bed was already empty. I don't know why he would have just up and left," Alexandria said with a slightly anxious expression. "And without even a clue of where he could have gone, I could not go and look for him. I am sure he will be back soon. He knows we do not intend to stay in town longer than needed."

The pained look on his face last night resurfaced in Fi's mind. She tried to reassure herself it had nothing to do with him overhearing the conversation between her and Iam. The timing of his absence would not ease the guilt in her heart.

There was no more room for emotions in Fi's mind. Erlan was a grown man, and he knew how to handle himself. For now, she had to address the things that could be handled.

"How is Iam doing this morning?" Fi turned her attention to Nin as she spoke. She hoped he would be well enough to leave Windcall soon. After the incident with the crowd yesterday, she didn't want to test their luck by overstaying the welcome. The longer they stayed, the more trouble they could cause for Nin.

"He is doing better than to be expected. He won't be able to ride a horse for another week or so, but I think he will make a full recovery. It was a good thing you got him to me when you did. I don't know how much longer that salve would have been able to keep that wound together. Without it, he would have been past the point of mending." Nin smiled at Fi as she answered before returning to her work.

While Fi was relieved he would recover, a week was a long time for them to stay in one place. Not only did they need to find more information to defeat Syler, the longer they stayed, the more likely her mark would be found out.

She had no real control over her powers yet and, with the anger she felt yesterday, she was worried. If there was another situation like the other day, who's to say she wouldn't be able to stay in control. It was only because Nin had intervened that she did not roast the crowd. They had to find a way to safely move Iam and get moving towards Adonia.

"Is there any way we could travel with him in his current state? I hate to push his health more than we should but, after yesterday, we should not stay here," Fi asked. She did not want to reveal they had any other agenda. As great as Nin had been to them, she knew the truth could not be shared. Nin's brows furrowed together as she considered Fi's request.

"While I do not suggest traveling, if you must, I have a litter behind the clinic," Nin said after a brief silence, "It's one of the older ones, but it should do the trick. You would need to ride slowly, however, as to not jostle him too much. Again, I suggest waiting here in town, but I cannot keep you prisoner."

Fi nodded in understanding. If the circumstances were different in any other way, she would heed her words. Looking to Alexandria, the same understanding reflected at her. They knew as well they needed to leave, and they needed to do it soon.

"Wait, what about Erlan? We cannot leave town without him," Selain said. The guilt in Fi's chest rose again. In trying to figure out the situation with Iam, Erlan slipped from her thoughts. Fi walked over to the window and glanced out towards the central square. There was no sign of him that she could see.

"I don't know where he could have gone. I would say he just went to go get something to eat, but I doubt that would go over well here in town. We can wait for him as long as possible, but we need to leave while it is still light out," Alexandria spoke up.

"And what if he isn't back before we need to leave? Are you suggesting we leave him behind?" Fi turned quickly, facing Alexandria. Her green eyes wide with surprise at the idea. Seeing a disagreement between them, Nin excused herself out back to check on the litter she offered.

"Not if we can help it. But you know as well as I do, we cannot stay here much longer. We must keep going and follow the plan. If we stay here too long, you may lose control, and he could discover who and where you are," Alexandria said, her jaw tensing while she kept her voice low. "He knows where it is we are heading. Whenever he is done doing whatever it is that has preoccupied him, he will know where to find us."

A knot formed in the pit of Fi's stomach. She did not like the idea of leaving without him but knew what Alexandria said to be the truth. All she could do was nod in agreement as her words failed her. Almost in a daze, she made her way around the clinic, collecting possessions that were theirs to be packed. Every five minutes or so she would glance at the door, willing it to open and Erlan to walk through.

Hours passed and there was no sign of him in the square out front. She grew nervous now. While he may have wanted some air or to run an errand, Fi thought he would have been back by now. He had not even left a note for them, so he must not have thought he would be gone long.

Looking around, she was apparently not the only one to have these thoughts. Selain was near the back of the shop, seeming to plead with Alexandria. Her bright red hair swaying as she shook her head, clearly stating they needed to leave. Alexandria wanted to leave over an hour ago but gave into the pleas of both Selain and Fi. Fi knew they could not wait any longer if they wished to have any light while they traveled.

"We have to trust he will find us," Fi said while she placed a hand on Selain. "Remember, Erlan is an amazing tracker. He will be able to follow us, no problem." Fi held her voice steady, trying to comfort Selain. In truth, she wondered what could have happened to him and feared the worst. After everything, however, Fi knew she had to be strong. The girl who ran in a panic a week ago could no longer be who she was.

Selain said no more as they packed up the horses. Aranya was tied to Verca so she could be led next to Selain. This was another battle, as Alexandria wanted to leave her behind in case Erlan needed to ride her. It was finally decided not to risk losing her entirely, and Aranya was brought along.

Without Erlan's help, it took both Fi and Selain to help Alexandria get Iam onto the litter. He was awake and livelier at this point.

"You know, when I imagined being handled by three beautiful women, this was not what I had in mind," Iam joked with a wink. The look that crossed Alexandria's face gave a clue she was arguing with herself about whether to drop him or not. He was lucky she decided the latter, and he was safely loaded.

Once he was secured, the three of them ensured their horses were loaded, and they did not miss anything. Every few minutes either Fi or Selain would glance around, hoping to catch a glimpse of the long chestnut hair that belonged to Erlan. They were only met with disappointment as they finally mounted their horses.

They began their ride in silence. The weight of their missing companion weighing heavily on their minds. It was the feeling of abandonment that hit Fi. Her chest felt as though all its contents had been replaced with lead. For all they knew, he was in trouble, hoping they would come to his aid. And here they were, riding off away from him.

"He will be alright, you know. For an elf, he is pretty tough. I saw him during the battle with the wolves. He is definitely someone I would want to have on my side in battle again." Iam said, seeing the worry on their faces. Selain nodded back to him, knowing his skill in battle.

"He is right. Erlan's skill in battle was one of the best in Pirn. He never joined with the other warriors but, if he wanted to, he could have been the top archer Pirn had to offer," Selain said, sitting up proudly. Whether this boast was at all true or to ease the heartache, Fi was not sure.

Having left later than Alexandria had wanted, the sun had begun its descent only a few hours after they had left Windcall. The blue, lightly clouded sky deepened in its hue. A grimace appeared on Alexandria's face as she peered at it. They continued riding on in silence as the blue turned an inky purple against the bit of orange left in the sky.

"I would have liked to have been further before we made camp today," Alexandria said to no one in particular. She scanned the path ahead of them, looking for a safe place to make camp. The light was almost completely gone to them, so they needed to find a spot quickly. "There, behind that set of trees."

She led them to a small patch of wayward pines that would provide some cover. Setting out their bedrolls, they made their camp without a fire, in fear it would attract attention. Though that provided its safety, it also left them open to an attack from the darkness should they be discovered. This required them to take shifts in listening to the darkness.

Knowing she would not be able to stay awake long, Fi requested the final shift that would lead into morning. Fi worried for another night without sleep, but her body had been so worn she was asleep before her head fully hit the comfort of her bedroll.

It felt all too soon that Selain was waking her for her turn to keep watch. Her eyes barely opened into slits to see who it was shaking her awake. It took a deal more effort to open them fully and push herself into a sitting position. She could barely make out the outline of Selain moving over to her bedroll.

Sitting in almost pitch dark played with her senses. She was surrounded by the sounds of buzzing bugs that blended to constant, dull noise. There was no way to distinguish one bug from another, even if she wanted to. But it wasn't the bugs getting to hear. Rustling sounds around in the dark were off-putting. Fi rationalized it was most likely raccoons, badgers, or a fox hunting for their next meal.

As morning loomed closer, the weather shifted quickly. When they first made camp, the air was warm and humid. Not to an uncomfortable degree but enough for one to notice. The air pressure was not dropping, and the wind had begun to pick up. When the sun should have been greeting them, they were met with dark clouds and rain.

The sky poured its contents onto Abaddon in reckless abandon. The wind's howl was haunting and chilled Fi more than the rain itself. Great crashes rang through the sky, following the sky lit ablaze. Lucky for them, the pines they chose kept them mostly dry. It was not until the wind blew hard enough that the rain was able to fully penetrate the dense needles of the pine. Selain was able to quickly make them a fire despite the wetness around them. Though it may have attracted attention, they would be no good cold or sick.

"Here," Fi said, laying another blanket over Iam, who still lay in the litter. He was already weak from healing, and it would be made worse if he got sick. As the sky rattled, her whole body tensed. Of all the things Fi was still afraid of from childhood, it was storms. She couldn't remember exactly why, but every storm filled her with fear.

"Hey, are you okay?" Iam covered the hand, lowering the blanket with his and squeezed. "It's just a bit of a storm. There isn't anything to fear." Instinctively, she squeezed his hand back in an attempt to gain comfort at that moment. After the sky quieted again, she opened her eyes and quickly pulled her hand back.

"Sorry, I uh, need to check on the horses," she said quietly and moved away before he could say anything else. Now is not the time for any of that. The horses were huddled together under one of the pines. They appeared alert from the storm but otherwise fine. She leaned against Hero, seeking the comfort of his familiar scent. The storm pressed on well into the night, putting them even further behind where they should have been. Things were not going well for them so far, and they had only just begun their journey.

Chapter 15

In the morning, the sky was a dim dark gray still holding remnants of the storm before. The air thick with moisture, which made breathing harder than normal. None of them appeared to have slept well through the storm. Dark circles adorned everyone's eyes as fatigued enveloped them all.

After a meager breakfast, they packed up their horses in an attempt to get back on course to Adonia. Fi was not quite sure how long they had until they reached its borders. Before she left Baydell, she was sure they would have ridden long enough to have been there when they reached Windcall. It never crossed her mind how little she knew about her world until now.

Since packing the horses, Selain never stopped looking over their shoulder as they rode. Her eyes were deep in emotion as she scanned the tree line. Her eyes desperately searched for any movement that could be Erlan. Worry and panic had set in the farther they rode from Windcall.

"Selain! You need to keep your eyes on the trail ahead of us!" Alexandria shot back as Iam was almost trampled by Verca. "I understand you are worried, but it does us no good if you injure those of us that are still here." Selain hung her head and turned back towards the trail ahead, not bringing herself to look back again.

Fi knew the farther she got away from Windcall, especially after the storm, the harder it would be for Erlan to track them. She left the worrying for now up to Selain. Her focus had to be on what they would do once they reached Adonia.

A hidden group of wizards was not going to be an easy thing to find. With their lives on the line, they would go out of their way and do who knows what to keep their village a secret. They also could not go into towns and begin asking questions. That was a sure-fire way to raise suspicion on their party. There had to be an option she was missing. A direction they could take that did not raise any alarms.

The ground beneath their feet had turned to mud from the storm and further slowed their travel time. At this juncture, any progress forward was something to be happy about. Iam's litter sank at the bottom, leaving a thick gouge in the ground behind Zephyr. At least it would give Erlan something to track.

As the day waded on, the sky peeked behind the clouds. While the clouds themselves were still dark and foreboding, streams of sunlight took their chance of freedom racing to shine on the ground below. Warmth filled Fi's body as she passed through a sun-filled patch. Opening her arms, she aimed to take in as much of the sun as it would offer. She was not sure the rain was done with them yet.

After three days of travel, their horses struggled up a steep hill as the mud slid beneath their hooves. Once they crested the peak, a city lay before them. This was the first time in her life Fi had laid eyes on Dracden, her country's capital. From where she stood, Fi could make out two large stone walls encircling the city. The buildings and homes inside would be surely protected from any outside dangers. At the far end sat what appeared to be an oversized building and was clear, even from a distance.

The castle had yet another wall around what was open to the city grounds. Four turrets connected where the walls would turn to allow the walls to encircle the castle. If Fi had to guess, there were guards stationed at every turret, watching for any signs of danger. One of these outer walls had an opening built into it. Most likely, this was how anyone the king received would enter.

The castle itself had high walls with turrets at every corner. The stone bricks were deep orange and dappled with lighter peach tones. Of all the buildings she could see, it was the most cared for. There had to be at least four levels to the castle. Fi could not even begin to imagine how many rooms would be inside.

From where she stood, she could make out the field of deep green on the flags blowing in the wind. Once they were closer, they would be able to make out the stark white dragon that adorned them. This was the emblem of Soeric. Being the country known for its militia power, it only made sense to have a strong symbol of strength.

Everyone had to slowly follow the path down the side of the hill. Every so often one of the horse's hooves would slip slightly, reminding them of the risk they were took descending after the storm. As they reached the bottom, it appeared everyone released the breaths they were subconsciously holding. The ground was now level, and the immediate danger of falling had passed.

While stopping in Dracden to rest was tempting, they had already lost too much time and needed to press on. Alexandria led them around the city on a smaller trail avoiding the main road. There was no need to attract attention from the guards that were surely posted on the city walls.

Seeing the burnt-orange city walls as they traveled was almost like the city itself teased them. Fi's mind drifted to the thought of warm soft beds to sleep in. The cold, hard ground last night left her body sore and stiff. Inside the walls would also be hot and fresh food. Most likely cooked to perfection by those skilled in the art of it. She learned quickly last night that no one in their party possessed those skills. At least none currently present.

Selain must have been having similar thoughts of food as Fi could hear her stomach growl, and she came up alongside her. The once perky and talkative elf was now quiet, her deep cerulean eyes staring daggers into Alexandria's back. There was no doubt about the reason. Selain made it clear she blamed Alexandria for Erlan being left behind. Fi's heart told her it had more to do with her.

The overall morale of the group was low. After many failed attempts to lift their spirits, even Iam grew quiet. The weather seemed to have read their emotions and shifted to taunt them more. The beams of sun that Fi had been enjoying were closed completely by dark clouds hanging low in the sky. They were in for another bit of rain if the Goddess had her say.

For hours, the silence continued between them all. The only thing Fi could hear was the sound of horses' hooves crunching the fallen leaves below them and their breathing. An autumn breeze blew lightly at her back. Pieces of her blonde hair had escaped her braid mid-ride and tickled at her face. This was truly a miserable trip so far, and she feared what still lay ahead of them if they had not even left Soeric yet.

By late afternoon, they had to stop to eat. If they continued the way they were, their stomachs would alert every Fiend in the area. Alexandria found what she deemed a secure spot, and they all dismounted. Fi's legs were stiff from all the riding they had been doing these almost two weeks. She was used to riding Hero, but it never was more than a few hours at a time.

In no time, Selain had a small fire going for them, and they were able to cook a meal. Though *cooking* was not a term Fi would use. The last stew Selain had prepared them had to be choked down. The smell reminded her of sweaty feet. It was only eaten out of necessity. Selain, however, thoroughly enjoyed what she had made and quickly ate three servings.

While she worked on her latest concoction, Fi stretched, trying to regain feeling in areas that had begun to go numb. She walked around, hoping to return circulation to her thighs and calves. She also had some personal business she needed to attend to.

"I'll be right over here," she called to the group, not wanting to go into detail. Once finished, she made her way back to the group when she heard a stick behind her *snap*. She froze, hoping it was just a squirrel or a deer passing through. Another snap came from behind her, and she whirled around.

There before her stood a Fiend. Its body was the darkest shade of black Fi had ever laid eye on. It was no question on how they were able to sneak up on their prey in the night. The only part of the Fiend that had a semblance of color was its white eyes that showed no signs of life. Its snake-like body was coiled on the ground. The serpentine face held two large fangs that dripped what could only be venom. On the tip of its tail sat a sharp barb.

It rose as some snakes do into a striking position. As it did,

Fi got a better idea of its full size. Uncoiled, it had to be at least seven feet long and could easily swallow her whole if so inclined. Fi felt frozen on the spot. Her mind told her muscles to move and run in the other direction, but they would not respond. The Fiend kept eye contact with Fi.

The Fiend began its attack by swinging its tail. Fi tried so hard to run or even close her eyes, but her body continued to betray her. As the barb quickly came closer, the Fiend suddenly recoiled. As it did, the eye contact between it and Fi was broken. She fell to the ground as her muscles gave out, and she closed her dry eyes.

As she looked up, she saw an arrow sticking out of the Fiend's side body where green leaked from the wound. It was not dead and came for Fi once again, not seeming to want to give up on what it deemed was prey. Now that Fi could move, she could run, but she was tired. She could not run forever.

It was easier to do that any other time and this time, she took control of it. A flame burst forth in her hands. As soon as it did, she threw the flame at the Fiend that had quickly closed the gap towards her. The flame hit it square in the face, and it reeled back in pain, emitting a ghastly noise akin to a scream. Another arrow came out of nowhere and drove home through one of its milky white eyes. It fell to the ground with a thickening *thud*, and Fi, too, collapsed to the ground.

She quickly looked around to find who it was that shot the arrow that saved her life. Every shadow became suspect, and she started to think she imagined the whole thing. Yet, two arrows with red feathers sat deep in the Fiend's hide, proving someone had saved her.

"Hello? Who's out there?" she called out, hoping they were truly there to save her and not take her for themselves.

"You know, I'll give it to you guys, you know how to cover your tracks well." The voice made Fi's heart pick up the pace. She knew that voice, and it was one she had hoped to hear for too long.

"Erlan!" She turned back around towards camp, and Erlan stood there, giving her the same smile he had for years. Her heart nearly flew from her chest when she saw his state. His face was covered in bruises, and his tunic was ripped and torn in many places. Her eyes quickly went from excitement to concern. "Oh, my goddess. What happened to you?!"

"I'm okay, I promise. I, uh, ran into some trouble when I went to get some air that night." His eyes turned slightly down as he finished his sentence. Fi knew why he went out that night, and him running into whatever he did was her fault.

"I'm so sorry. Why did you leave? You knew the people of WIndcall were out for blood. Whatever made you leave the safety of the clinic?" Tears welled in her eyes. She told herself she was done crying and being weak, but she couldn't stop them now.

"I am the one who should be sorry," Erlan said. "It was irresponsible for me to up and leave the clinic. At the minimum, I should have provided you all with a note." He did not answer the question. Fi was not sure if he was avoiding it or too busy with the apology.

"Why did you leave, Erlan?" Fi asked him again. She wanted an answer if for some reason it was something she didn't want to hear.

"Fi, I have known you your entire life," Erlan said. "We have always been close, and I held you and Byron as my deepest friends. I have always wanted to protect you, and I thought it was because of the secret I had sworn to once I came of age to hold it.

Fi's heart broke at the word friend. She had been right in how he thought of her. How could he see her as anything else after all these years? She waited for Erlan to finish explaining.

"Something about what Iam said to you bothered me. I couldn't shake knowing how he felt about you. His story just didn't add up. There were too many coincidences for it all to track. But I couldn't figure out what his angle might have been. Though part of me began wondering if it was jealousy I was feeling. It is not an emotion I am accustomed to. I needed some air to clear my head and figure out for sure what was bothering me."

Fi waited for him with bated breath to finish his story. To explain how he had gotten those injuries after leaving before asking the question she wanted to ask so desperately. It was not until she realized she stopped breathing altogether did she draw breath.

"What did you decide?" Before Erlan could answer, Selain's voice came from behind Fi. The two of them quickly moved away from one another.

"Fi! Hello, are you over here?" Selain came upon them at that moment and saw the two of them and the slain and burned Fiend behind them. "Erlan?! Are you okay? Where the hell have you been, and why is there a Fiend out in the middle of the day?"

Chapter 16

Fi's mind ran a mile a minute. The mood in the air quickly shifted from one direction to another in the blink of an eye. She felt as though a bucket of cold water had been thrown over her. If Selain would not have called out when she did, the situation would be a lot more awkward for everyone rather than just herself. She knew she should have to finish the conversation with Erlan later, but now was not the time. Selain threw herself into Erlan's arms and hit him in the chest.

"You can't just do that! Taking off and not telling anyone! Especially in a human city that clearly wanted our heads just for existing. What in the hell were you thinking?!" The lecture continued until she was out of breath.

"I am sorry for worrying everyone. I felt stifled in the tiny clinic, so I went to get some fresh air," as he answered, his eyes flicked to Fi for just a moment before continuing. "Unfortunately, you were right. Taking a walk in Windcall was a mistake for the very reason you mentioned. I was walking along the tree line, enjoying the wildness of vegetation when some of the men from town approached me. I will spare you all the grim details, and though I bested them, they definitely got a good deal of hits in."

Selain looked at him closer without the blinding rage she had moments ago and saw the bruises on his face and the rips in his tunic. Tears welled in her eyes again as she gingerly inspected all of them for any signs of infection.

"You idiot," was all she said before she fell back into his chest, weeping in both relief and sadness for the state of his return. Erlan let her cry for a few minutes before turning their attention back to the dead Fiend that lay behind them.

"The Fiend on the other hand. What it is doing out in the morning hours, is beyond me. In my many years, I have never seen one leave wherever they sleep before the sun had completely set along the horizon. I am relieved I was able to find you all before it killed Fi." Erlan pulled away from Selain as he spoke. He went over to inspect the body more closely.

"I do appreciate you saving me yet again. There is something I do not understand. While I made eye contact with the Fiend I could not move. My body would not respond, nor could I even speak. Is that normal? I mean I knew about Fiends of course but have never come across one myself. Just heard stories," Fi spoke to Erlan. If anyone would know the answer, she was sure it would be him.

"That is not something I have heard happening to someone who has encountered a Fiend before. Granted, many do not live to tell tales after running into one." Erlan paused as he saw a strange mark upon the Fiend. A familiar outline of a flame was etched on the head of the Fiend. His heart sank into his chest as the realization came over him. The flame was the emblem of Highbarrow. "We need to get back to the others quickly. We are in danger the longer we stay still."

The three of them made haste back to the campsite where Erlan quickly informed everyone of his findings. Alexandria smothered the flames of their campfire with dirt so to lessen the smoke that could be seen. Everyone else broke down camp and packed all provisions back into the saddlebags of the horses. They were all surprised to see Iam up and packing Ithil.

"What are you doing? Get back in the litter!" Fi exclaimed, stopping her tasks. "You are not yet fully healed, and we do not need you bleeding as you did before."

"I appreciate the concern but, honestly, I cannot ride in that litter any longer. It really is bad for the back," he said with a smile. "I am fine to ride, and the litter would only slow us down. Time and speed are important now." He finished tightening the closure on his saddlebag before turning and helping Selain, who had most of the food to pack in her saddlebags.

Though Fi did not like it, she knew he was right. They needed to focus on going forward and finding the wizard village in Adonia, if it even existed. There was a chance this rumor would not pan out, and they would be left with nothing more to go on and nowhere to turn.

Once they were ready, they fell into formation, keeping Fi securely between two others to keep her safe. With Fiends coming out during the day, the chance of danger heightened for them all. Fi knew this journey would be a dangerous one, but it seemed things kept finding them even though they were covering their tracks. First the wolves, and now the Fiend. She shook off the thought. She had never left Baydell how was she supposed to know what is normal and what is not.

The weather was still heavy as they followed the path that would lead them to the border. Though no rain, Fi could feel moisture collecting on her skin. It chilled her, though she wondered if it was a cumulation of the moisture and her nerves of what was to come.

After traveling for another three days without the clouds and precipitation letting up. Alexandria came to a stop at the crest of a hill. Stretching to the north and south stood large gray pillars every ten feet. Fi remembered Byron telling her these designated the end of one country and the beginning of the neighboring one.

"We are just about to cross into Adonia. We must be even more careful here than we were in Soeric. I blame no one for what happened in Windcall. In our country, elves have the right to be in the cities without persecution." Alexandria closed her eyes for a moment, then opened them again, looking pained. "In every other country, elves are persecuted. They can be killed on sight if found within their borders."

"That's horrible!" Selain said in disgust The burning ember of anger she had already held in her eyes intensified into a wildfire. "I knew they hated us, but to be killed instantly? What if it was a child who got lost? Are you saying that if an elvish child lost his way and accidentally crossed out of Soeric, their life is forfeit?" Selain trembled on her horse. Her voice had started as an outcry but grew into an outright yell. Tears welled in her eyes. Fi felt anger, too. It all seemed so wrong they would not even be given a chance.

"I can't imagine what that feels like," Iam said. His voice held slight anger to it. "It is what happened to me as I entered your village."

"And for that, we are sorry," Erlan said. "If I am to return to my village alive, I hope to make a change to the customs of Pirn pertaining to humans. It is not right we act in a way we also deem unfit for ourselves."

"I never said it was right how they handled when an elf

crosses the border. I do not agree that just because you are an elf you are automatically guilty of anything. I hope I have proven that to you on this journey. We have to be extremely cautious from now on," Alexandria said in hopes of calming the situation.

"I hate this. We didn't do anything yet are treated worse than..." Selain broke off, collecting her breath and wiping a tear that escaped her eye. Before she could speak again, Erlan moved Aranya closer and placed his hand on Selain's shoulder.

"It is as our parents warned us for many years. We never thought the worst because of where we lived. We have taken the freedoms in Soeric for granted. Now, we must always be careful and keep our hoods up. We cannot take any chances," Erlan said. He was the voice of reason between the two of them, and she let out a calming sigh.

"All of us here agree with you. And should anything happen, we will stand by your side." Fi attempted a reassuring smile, though her thoughts filled with doubt they would be enough to stop a whole country. Selain did not finish her thought, nor did she answer Fi. She only nodded and looked down at Verca's head, petting her mane.

Fi looked up to Alexandria, about to tell her they were ready to continue when she noticed the hue of the sky. The clouds had cleared and showcased a darkening sky before them. Night was probably not the time to cross into dangerous territory.

"Alexandria, we should probably make camp and travel in the morning to Adonia. I know we have to be more cautious and find the village, but we will be of no use if we are exhausted from riding. We should, however, sleep in shifts should anything try to attack us in the night," Iam said. "Now is not the time to be making hasty decisions."

It was agreed, and they made camp just far enough off the path to not be seen by anyone daring to travel. Shifts meant broken sleep, but it was more rest than if they had pressed on. Thankfully, nothing attacked them that night and, in the morning, they had the energy to safely continue into an unknown and dangerous country.

The further they traveled into Adonia, the more the terrain changed. The forests thinned out and, eventually, disappeared altogether. What was once lush soil grew hard, and the horses' hooves kicked up dust with each step they took. Without the forests, the wind whipped at them fiercely. Fi wondered how anyone could survive in an environment such as this. There was nowhere she knew of so desolate in Soeric.

By midday, the clouds thinned and revealed the azure sky above them. The light of the sun only illuminated the gloom. The further they traveled, the more depressed Fi felt. It was as if whatever sucked the life from the vegetation seeped into her. The thought of staying in a village with these surroundings was not something she looked forward to.

Once the noon hour had passed, they could see what looked to be a small city come into view. The buildings were made from worn stone. The wind had eroded some of them over time. They were placed close together, most likely to limit the wind whipping through the city. There were no paved streets, just the same dirt they had been walking on to get there.

Before entering the town, Erlan and Selain ensured their hoods were raised and held tightly so they would not fly off and reveal their race. It was not something any of them were happy about but, unfortunately, it was a necessity to keep them and everyone else safe.

The city appeared lifeless as they rode in. There was no one on the streets or any movement from the windows. The only signs of life were horses tied up outside some of the buildings, with the walls on either side of the long wood ties to block the wind. The horses must have been used to the winds, as they did not seem to mind it.

The building with the most horses outside of it ended up being the tavern. All of them tied up their horses to a worn log, ensuring they were tied securely. Feeling guilty about leaving him in the current weather, Fi petted Hero's neck apologetically before heading into the tavern.

Fi was grateful to be out of the wind and inside the warm building. It looked as rough on the inside as it did on the outside. None of the chairs matched at the tables they were placed at. And there were a good many of them broken in one way or another. Hanging on the walls were strange paintings with symbols Fi had never seen before. One looked similar to a spiral, but it trailed off in the end to a crooked triangular shape. Another appeared to have been done by a child for, no matter how long Fi stared at it, she could not figure out what it was.

The beams of the tavern were exposed on every wall and the ceiling. Even behind the stone, the wind could be heard whipping outside. The building would creak every now, and then when a large gust would come through.

Surrounding some of the tables were tough-looking men. Many had disheveled beards, and their hair looked as though it had not been brushed in days. Granted, that could easily have been from the walk over to the tavern. They wore basic tunics and breeches that were tattered and worn. The group eyed them suspiciously as they entered the tavern and found five mismatched chairs at a table.

"I wonder where we are?" Selain whispered. "This isn't a place I would like to stay too long if we can help it." She looked around the tavern before pulling tightly on her hood, keeping it over her ears.

"There is no way we can continue travel in this wind. Unless it dies down, we may have to be here for the night. If we can grab some rooms for the night, we can hole up in them until we are able to leave," Alexandria said, leaning in towards Selain. "It is not ideal, but we must make safety our priority. We do not know anyone in Adonia, nor can we trust anyone outside our group."

"I understand. I just hate acting as though I am a criminal hiding from the law," Selain replied before leaning away, examining the room again. Her eyes caught sight of the bartender, and he made his way over to the table.

He stood at an easy six feet and was built bigger than Byron, which said something. The bartender's beard was slightly better kept than his patrons, though could still use a going over with a brush. His shoulder-length hair was a sooty black, yet there were streaks of gray shooting through it. His beard was the complete opposite. It was comprised mainly of an iron-gray with only a little black left in it. As he approached the table, his smiles caused wrinkles to appear around his amber-brown eyes.

"Welcome to Moburn. I have not seen you all before. I am Holm. What can I get for you?" he asked. His voice was low and gruff. There was an air of command around him, and Fi determined he was not someone to be on the wrong side of.

"Four ales and a water, please," Iam answered, returning Holm's smile with his own. "Also, is there any idea how long this wind will last? We were hoping to continue our journey after a rest."

"Sorry to tell you that this storm won't break till morning. They usually last three to four days, and we are currently on the fourth. It looks as though you will be staying with us tonight if you are smart not to travel," Holm answered, his smile drooping slightly. He glanced over to two men at a table, both staring over at them.

"Two rooms would be sufficient. How much do we owe you?" Iam answered, peering at the two men before returning his gaze to Holm.

"Two silver for the pair of them," he answered. Alexandria pulled two silver from her coin purse and handed it over to Holm. "If I were you, I would keep a close eye on the ladies here. Not to spook them, but we do not see many beautiful ladies come through here, and you brought three." He then turned and walked away to fill their drink order.

Fi glanced over her shoulder again at the two men, who smiled at her. Though she assumed they were attempting to be friendly, Fi felt no warmth from them. It was as though they were wolves smiling at the sheep they intended to eat for dinner.

Chapter 17

A few rounds of drinks were consumed while they finally ate a hot meal. There was not much in the way of vegetables, but the meat offered was edible. All of it was better than eating jerky or foraged food. And really, anything was better than food cooked by Selain.

The whole time they were eating, Fi felt eyes on her back. When she finally turned around, she saw two patrons quickly turn their heads down when they made eye contact. The one on the left was a large burly man. His shoulder-length hair and long unkept beard rivaled the red in Alexandria's. His shoulders were set wide, but he did not thin out in the middle. An obvious ale gut hung over his pants.

The other man at the table was smaller than his companion. His hair was an ash-blond and cut short. When he tilted his head to see if Fi was still looking, a scar was evident across his face. It started at his forehead and curved down his face. A small chill went up Fi's spine, and she quickly turned around back to her table.

After they placed the horses in a proper stable and got them something to eat, they squared themselves away in their rooms. The storm outside died down as Fi could no longer hear it roar through the walls. They still had to stay the night as it was too dark for them to travel safely in unknown lands.

Iam and Erlan were in one room while Alexandria, Selain, and Fi were in another. The room was shabby and only had two beds. The beds were small and could only comfortably hold one person. Though *comfortable* was a generous way to describe them. The blankets on the bed were dark brown, worn, and itchy. Selain and Fi opted not to use the blankets and laid their bedrolls on top of the bed.

Alexandria had opted to take the bedroll on the floor so Selain and Fi could have the beds. There was a slight debate before Selain and Fi conceded. Between the two beds was a small wooden table that had nicks from what Fi could imagine was from knives. Why someone would shove their knives into a table was beyond her.

"So, Fi, what is up with you and Iam?" Selain asked as she flopped onto the bed, kicking dust into the air. Fi could not figure out why Selain cared so much about what was between them. She began to wonder if Selain had ulterior motives for pushing them together.

"What do you mean?" Fi asked through a torrent of coughs from the dust. Her mind had been on what Erlan almost said, which made her completely forgotten about what had transpired with Iam. Why did this all have to be happening right now? Her mind had other things it needed to be concerned with.

"I hate to sound like an eavesdropper, but I was awake when Iam professed his feelings for you," Selain said quietly. Fi's stomach made a flop inside her. Alexandria made no sounds but had stopped cleaning her sword to listen better.

"Oh...that. I really do not know what to say to him. I mean, in all honesty, I do not know him that well to even decide right now. Besides..." She replied. She wanted to say it did not matter anyway because she felt for someone else. But of all people, the worst thing to say that to was Selain.

"Besides *what*? Do you have someone back home you had to leave behind or something?" Selain probed, trying to get the information from Fi. She could not respond, no words coming to her mouth to cover her almost-confession. Thankfully, Alexandria came to her rescue.

"She means it doesn't really matter right now as other things are more important than who to give her heart to. She wants to focus on the task at hand and not get sidetracked, right?" Alexandria shot over her shoulder as she resumed cleaning her sword before placing it in the scabbard. Whether Alexandria knew the truth or not, she gave Fi a way out of the situation.

"Exactly," Fi said quickly. "Now is not the time to be thinking about a relationship. We still have no idea which direction we need to go to find the village, let alone if it even exists. My brain is too full of everything else to even be thinking about that. He will just have to deal with things being one-sided. Now, if you'll excuse me, I need a glass of water."

Fi quickly stood and slipped out the door before either of them could say another word. She felt overwhelmed again and just needed to separate herself and clear her head. As she made her way down the stairs towards the tavern below, she heard two men's voices. She pressed herself against the stairwell wall, trying to disappear.

"I seriously need to move out of this desolate country. If you are not working in the healing medicine trade, there is not a lot for you to do to make a good living," one gruff voice said.

"You have been saying that for years. Just do it already. If you really cannot stand your job at the trading store, just pick up and go already. Otherwise, quit your bitching," another said back, his voice deeper than the first.

"If I had the money, you think I wouldn't. I mean, if the women in the other countries look like the three who came in tonight, I may go broke and move tomorrow," the gruff voice responded. Fi's heart dropped into her stomach as she tried to press herself further into the wall. It was just then Fi remembered Holm saying the three of them should not be off alone. She had to sneak back to her room.

"Yeah, those three were lookers. Though that long-haired blonde had a look of innocence about her, if you know what I mean. Too bad they were not traveling alone, right?" he said with a laugh.

Fi felt sick to her stomach hearing them talk about her that way. She turned to sneak away, and the stair squeaked in betrayal. As it did, she let out an audible gasp. She clamped her hands over her mouth quickly, but the noise had already escaped her mouth.

"What was that?" the deep voice asked. Footsteps raced up the stairs, and she attempted to make her way back to her room. Before she got up the second flight of stairs, a firm hand grabbed her wrist and spun her around.

She was thrust into the arms of a man with a burned orange beard that tickled her face and reeked of ale. Wide-eyed, she looked up to see his charcoal-gray eyes devoid of emotion staring into hers. Fi fought him, but he was much stronger than she was. His grip tightened on her wrist the more she fought.

"Hey, Jasper. This is the one you were going on about, ain't it?" the gruff voice said, turning to an ash-blond man. It was the men who had been staring at the table all night.

"It's like the goddess herself smiled on me today. Hey, Tobias, why don't you pass that beauty over here," Jasper said, a sneer appearing across his scarred face. With that, Fi was thrown like a rag doll into the arms of the waiting man.

"Let go of me!" Fi exclaimed, and a hand clamped over her mouth. If she was scared before, she was terrified now. She knew what these men's intentions were and wasn't ready to go quietly.

"Ho, oh, she is a feisty one there, Jasper. Better be careful with her." Tobias laughed.

Fi knew no one was going to save her this time. Selain and Alexandria thought she was getting water, and Iam and Erlan had no idea she had even left the room. She had to take care of herself for once. It was up to her to get herself out of the situation she put herself into.

She tried to fight Jasper again, but his grip tightened into more of a bear hug, and she could not move. With one choice left, she tried to bring on the burning feeling that would lead to the fire she could bring forth. No matter how hard she tried, though, the sensation would not come. There was a spark, but it would not grow into a flame.

Jasper pulled his hand off her mouth and crushed her lips beneath his own. Fi kicked him in the leg, trying to get him to let go. Why couldn't she conjure the flame she could easily produce in Windcall? In that moment, Fi felt as hopeless as she had ever felt. She did not have the physical strength to fight them off, nor could she find a way to produce fire.

Jasper continued to kiss her as Tobais ran his hands through her platinum hair. Terror soon overtook her as these men caressed her. Suddenly there was then a new sensation came over Fi. The spark in her body crackled and popped inside her. Her body buzzed and visibly vibrated in Jasper's arms.

"Aw, don't be scared, sweetheart. I promise I will be real gentle," Jasper said, breaking the kiss, mistaking her vibrations for shakes of fear. Those were the last words he spoke before a resounding *boom* sounded, and both men dropped to the ground, twitching. Fi looked down and saw sparks still coming from her fingers. An intense wave of nausea came over her.

Her head shot up as doors banged open and footsteps charged her direction. No one could discover whatever it was she just did to these men. She quickly crouched, as if in fear of whatever made the noise. Her breath quickened to better feign fear. Though her heart beat so fast, she did not have to try hard.

"What the hell was that?!" Holm called from the bottom of the stairs. This was followed by a muddle of other voices, making it hard to discern their answers. She looked through her fingers to see her entire party and a few other guests on the landing. Her entire party called out her name, but it was Alexandria who got their first.

"Fi, are you alright?" Alexandria quickly checked her over. Fi nodded because, besides the intense feeling of nausea, she was fine physically.

Alexandria kneeled and placed her fingers on the necks of the two men. Where a pulse should have been sat still. Alexandria hung her head before turning back to Fi in a hushed tone. "If this was you, just nod slowly." Again, Fi nodded. Selain, Iam, and Erlan reached them then.

"Are you alright?" Fi was bombarded by all of them. This was followed by questions about the men who laid around her. She could not talk about it, not here, not in front of everyone. It was horrible, and she was not ready to relive it now.

"Can someone tell me what is going on here?" Holm said as he broke their bombardment of questions. "I am curious as to what this young woman was doing out here, and why Jasper and Tobias are laying here. And what that god-awful noise was." Everyone looked at each other and tried to come up with an explanation to give him. Alexandria placed a hand on Fi's shoulder before standing and pushing her fiery red hair back over her shoulder.

"I would like to know something, too. It appears your two patrons here ganged up on my friend. What their intent was, I will leave it to your imagination because I do not think I could say it aloud. And during this altercation, some loud noise came through, and the men fell to the ground, dead. Is there something about this place we should know about? Why are you so willing to allow men like this to stay here?" Alexandria bombarded him with accusations. As if it was his fault that Fi was attacked and something in the inn caused the noise.

"I don't know what you are suggesting, young lady, but had I known they would actually attack her, I would not have permitted them to stay here. And there is nothing in this inn besides the people you see here and the furniture," he said back, sounding offended.

"Then why is it you told us not to let the women walk off on their own? You had to have known something," Iam said through gritted teeth, his jaw taut.

"I said that because those two had not seen a woman in a good long time and did not want any unwanted advances. I did not think they would go and attack the poor girl," he said with remorse in his voice. "But I have no idea what would have caused such a sound. It is unlike anything I have ever heard.

"I do not know what it was, either, but my poor friend has

been through enough tonight. If you all are done with this, I would like to get her back to our room," Selain said, putting her hand on Fi's shoulder helping her stand.

No one argued with Selain, but those outside the group eyed her warily. They did not fully trust where the sound came from. However, without being able to prove anything, they had no choice but to let them pass.

They walked Fi up the stairs, with Iam and Erlan staring back at the two men on the ground with hatred in their eyes. Walking down the hallway, Fi's whole body felt heavy. Every step felt like there was mud beneath her feet. All she wanted was to get back to her room, lay down, and forget about what happened tonight.

Chapter 18

Fi had kept her composure the entire length of the hallway back to the bedroom. There was no need to raise the level of suspicion already thrown in her direction. As the door to the room opened, however, Fi flew inside and threw herself on her bed. The weight of taking a life, even those that meant to harm her, weighed heavily on her.

Deep down, she had known it could happen. It was more than likely to happen. It just did not occur to her to consider how she would feel. She was not prepared for the feeling of guilt. Like she was cruel for deciding the fate of another person's life. She also felt dirty from being touched in that way by a man. A part of her was forever changed after tonight. She knew that she could never go back to who she was before the night the mark burned in her skin.

She heard the door quickly close behind her as the tears fell from her eyes. She did not try to stop them, as crying now was almost cathartic. Having held in so much had taken a toll, and she needed a release. A hand touched back, and she turned to see Alexandria.

"Fi, what happened? Did they hurt you? Are you okay?" Alexandria asked her. Fi knew that Alexandria had good intentions, but she did not want to think about it, let alone talk about it. But she had to let them know about the sparks from her fingers. There was a new manifestation of her magic, and they had to know about it. She slowly sat up, not making eye contact with anyone in the room. She felt dirty all over.

"I went to get a drink of water, so I headed to the bar downstairs to see if Holm was still down there," Fi answered. Her voice shook, and she sniffed every so often to keep from crying. "I got mostly down the stairs when I heard the two men talking about…things that do not matter. They must have heard me because they came up the stairs quickly. And then they, um…" Fi stopped. This was the part she couldn't bear to think about. How was she supposed to tell them this? Her first kiss was stolen from her by a vile man she murdered.

"It's okay, Fi," Iam said, walking over and grabbing her hand while sitting on the bed next to her. "Whatever happened, you know we are on your side." The comfort in his voice gave Fi the courage to continue. She squeezed his hand as she continued and did not notice Erlan stiffen in the corner of the room as their hands embraced.

"They tried to have their way with me forcibly," Fi said, trying to get out the words before her brain stopped her. Everyone in the room seemed to have already had an idea of what had happened.

Iam's hand left hers and replaced itself around her shoulders. "I couldn't let them do it. I tried to conjure fire to singe them a little in hopes I would be able to get back to the room. As hard as I tried, nothing happened till the lightning. And they fell to the ground, and the sound filled the air. I didn't mean to kill them, I swear!" She sobbed again only, this time, into Iam's chest rather than the pillow.

"If you wouldn't have killed them, I would have," Iam, Erlan, and Alexandria said in unison. They all looked at each other, amused at their similar thinking.

"So, what do we do now?" Selain asked the room. "They can't prove Fi killed them so we won't be kicked out or have whatever they would deem authorities take her away. Should we just follow our plan and leave in the morning like nothing happened?"

"It's probably the best course of action," Alexandria said. "If we just disappeared in the night, they may send someone after us, and we can't have that happening. In the morning, we will keep to ourselves and leave as soon as possible. You guys should head back to your room for the night. We can watch over Fi here."

"If it is all the same to you, I would rather get my bedroll and stay in here. Last time we separated, Fi was left to walk a strange building alone," Erlan said, already moving to the door to retrieve his bedroll. Iam was in agreement and followed behind him. Ten minutes later, the five of them were crammed into the tiny bedroom.

Alexandria had placed her bedroll near the door, though she assured Fi it had nothing to do with someone coming in during the night. Between Selain and Fi's bed was where Erlan and his bedroll had been placed. While Iam's bedroll was between Fi's bed and the far wall of the room. It did not take long before the room became warm from all the bodies in such a small space.

Sleep did not come easy to Fi for yet another night during this journey. Every time she closed her eyes, all she saw were the faces of Jasper and Tobias staring at her, unmoving on the floor. Lying in the bed, she stared at the ceiling, trying to scrub her brain of the memories. From the other bed, Selain's snores were audible, and Fi envied the fact she could fall asleep.

Giving in to the fact sleep was not coming, Fi sat up to formulate their next move towards finding the wizard village. There was no way they could work for any information here in Moburn after what happened tonight. They had to decide in which direction they were going to travel. They were currently in the Northwestern part of Adonia. The best course of action would most likely be to head Southeast towards the capital, Rayacre.

Larger cities along the way could be dangerous with Erlan and Selain having to keep their hoods up, but there would be a better chance of blending in and trying to listen for information. She decided to pose her makeshift plan to everyone in the morning.

Fi laid back down in yet another attempt to sleep. The mattress below her was lumpy, and finding a position even in a good state of mind would be difficult. Staring at the door made her so nervous someone was going to come barreling in to take her away for murder. This caused her to turn towards the far wall and Iam, who stared at her. Fi nearly jumped out of the bed when she saw him awake.

"You sure do make a lot of noise when you can't sleep. Do you want to talk about it?" Iam whispered as he sat up in his bedroll. Fi shook her head, fighting back another round of tears as the subject she was trying to forget was brought back up. "Listen, I can't imagine what you are feeling. Well, I know the taking a life part, but not anything else." The cavalier way he talked about committing murder threw Fi for a loop.

"How can you be so calm about killing someone?" Fi said a little louder than she intended. It caused Erlan to stir next to her, but he did not wake up. "I cannot stop thinking about it. The scene keeps playing over and over in my head. It is a constant loop I cannot get out of." Her body shook as the tears escaped her eyes. Wiping her eyes, she swore the water beaded and gathered on her palm but, when she blinked, it was gone.

Iam quickly rose, joining Fi on the bed. He wrapped his arm around her, and she turned to sob into him yet again. The flood gates of her emotions had opened, and there was no shutting them now. Iam's shirt was soaked with her tears when her eyes finally dried up.

"Sorry about your shirt," she said, pulling away from him. A yawn escaped as her emotional release left her drained. She thought she may finally be able to sleep.

"It's okay, really. Do you at least feel better?" Iam asked her as he smiled. Fi nodded. A small weight had lifted now, and it was not so hard to carry the burden she had. As Iam moved back towards his bedroll, a feeling came over Fi, and she grabbed his sleeve.

"Please, don't leave yet. I don't want to be alone," she said quietly. Fi did not know what came over her, but the thought of lying in her bed alone was enough to keep her awake again. Her mind would wander and go back to the loop of earlier. "At least until I fall asleep."

Iam did not hesitate and laid beside her, wrapping his arm around her. A feeling of safety washed over Fi, and a deep, dreamless sleep overcame her. She welcomed it and finally fell asleep.

"I knew there was something going on!" Selain yelled, pulling Fi suddenly from her sleep. Iam must have fallen asleep because, as Fi woke, she felt the weight of his arm still on her. She shot up, quickly dislodging herself from Iam's embrace.

This caused him to wake and jump back out of the bed.

"No. No. No. I get how this looks, but I swear it is not what you think," Fi sputtered, glancing towards Erlan as she spoke, but he was not even looking at her. His eyes were fixed on Iam, and if looks could kill, Iam would have died where he stood.

"Really, because it looks like you two love birds moved into bed together after we all fell asleep," Selain said as she wiggled her eyebrows. Fi did not know how to respond. While she and Iam were not a thing, she had asked him to stay. Him being in her bed had been her decision.

"Fi was crying last night, and I was just trying to comfort her. I did not intend to fall asleep, but after traveling all day yesterday, I was exhausted. Like Fi said, it is not what you think," Iam stated. His denial was so believable. Fi was confused by the pain that hit her heart.

"Now is not the time for this discussion," Alexandria said, breaking into the conversation. "Our focus now needs to be getting food and getting back on the road. With the events of last night, we must leave Moburn as soon as we can. Can we please just pack up, eat breakfast, and leave." Everyone grew silent. Alexandria, as ever, was the voice of reason and made sure to keep everyone on task.

Without another word, everyone rolled up their bedrolls and packed their bags. Once everyone was squared away, they made their way down towards the tavern. They intended a quick breakfast and to head straight to the stables to retrieve their horses.

The tavern was almost empty as they came down. Only three other patrons shared a table on the other side of the room. The minute the party came down, they drew silent as stared. They then turned back to each other tightly and commenced their talking. Fi knew exactly what, or rather who, they were talking about.

Finding an open table, they all sat down. Fi and Iam made sure not to sit next to each other, putting Alexandria in between them. They then waited for Holm to come to them. After what seemed like a longer wait than it should have been, Holm came to the table.

"Can we get a few breakfast plates for the table, please?" Alexandria asked, sounding completely normal as Fi did not even attempt to make eye contact with Holm.

"I think you all should just leave," he said. Fi's body stiffened at them being kicked out of the tavern. As she looked up, Holm stood staring at her with his arms crossed defiantly, his brows furrowed, creating wrinkles on his face. A bit of anger burned in the pit of Fi's stomach. She may have committed a crime, but it was not as though the men were innocent.

"We understand. We will just go. I am sure we will be fine with the rations we have left." Alexandria stood when Holm sighed. The wrinkles on his forehead deepened.

"Well, I can at least send you all with some food to eat on the road. Give me just a minute," he said as he turned on his heel back into the kitchen. After ten minutes, he returned with a sack of bread and jerky. He placed it on the table in front of Alexandria and motioned for them towards the door. All of them stood and made their way back outside.

Their horses were already saddled and ready when they got to the stables. The whole town seemed ready for them to leave. Fi grabbed Hero's reins, walking him out of the stable and onto the road. He nudged her gently, seeming to know something was wrong.

"I'm okay, Hero," she said to him as she patted his neck. Her foot slipped into the stirrup, and she threw herself over Hero's back. The familiar feeling of sitting in his saddle relaxed her a bit. Going for rides with him on the farm or being around him was how she dealt with stress before.

"Can you tell us which direction to ride to reach Rayacre?" Alexandria asked the stable master. They were all in unknown lands, so they had no idea which direction they were to venture. They knew southeast but did not know which way that was from where they were now. The stable master seemed more than willing to give them directions to Rayacre.

The winds had died down and turned into a strong breeze. The surrounding landscape resembled a barren wasteland. There were dead and dried-up shrubs breaking through the hard ground. This led Fi to believe, at some point in the seasons, things could grow here. Even if it was enough to just break the ground and die.

While there were clouds in the sky to help shield them from the sun, the air was hot and uncomfortable. Fi sweated and took her outer layer of clothing off to her short-sleeved tunic. Unlike the day before, the wind was welcoming while they baked in the sun's gaze. When they were far enough away from Moburn, they felt they could talk freely to one another.

"So, with what happened, I am guessing you have two forms of magic now?" Selain asked, breaking the silence. Everyone looked at her, and she shrugged. "Fire and lightning, huh? I guess when they talk about destructive magic, they were talking literally. I thought they might have referred to controlling someone's mind. Now, that could get destructive."

"Who knows the limit of power one who has been marked can use. There is a chance this is just the beginning of it," Erlan responded. "Who knows what Fi is really capable of." Fi was not sure he was just talking about her powers. She felt the familiar pang of guilt she did in Windcall.

She thought back to the attack of the Fiend. It felt like it happened a lot longer ago than it truly had. Time seemed jumbled the farther they traveled. Erlan had begun to tell her something about what he wanted. It seemed important, but Fi feared what he meant to say. Now, he gave her the cold shoulder. It was almost insulting as she had done nothing wrong.

"Does anyone know what it is we are looking for?" Iam asked. "I know it is a village of hiding wizards, but it can't be that easy to find, right? I mean, they have been in hiding for a while according to the stories, so they must be doing something right."

No one could give him an answer. The only thing they knew for sure was they needed to get to Adonia. It was a mystery how they would make it the rest of the way successfully. Fi cursed, there were no directions for them to follow. This whole country was unknown territory, and they did not know what lay ahead.

Chapter 19

"This is becoming impossible!" Selain exclaimed, throwing her hands in the air.

They had been traveling for two weeks and were no closer to finding the village than when they started. As the sun set, they decided to make camp. There were no cities or towns nearby for them to attempt shelter in.

During the last two weeks, they had seen only one other city besides Moburn. The city of Terin was bigger than Moburn, which lent them hope of finding any kind of information. There were multiple taverns and shops for them to blend into for any word about the village they looked for.

The streets of Terin were comprised of the same dusty ground they had been traveling on their whole journey in Adonia. The city had not bothered to add pavement to travel on. Buildings were misshapen, hardened clay. They resembled mounds more than buildings. Fi was used to the cities in Soeric, being of finer construction.

Many shops lined the streets, and the group was able to replenish their stores. Alexandria utilized the blacksmith to sharpen her sword, while Erlan replenished his arrows. They stayed at three of the taverns on three different nights in Terin. Hoping to find a clue as to where they should begin looking.

The first two taverns, Hagleo and Forthe, reminded Fi of the one in Moburn. The floor was dirt, and the tables and chairs unmatching. Many of the patrons were deep into the drink and paid them no attention. The food was unflavored and almost made Fi wish for Selain's cooking. Once they choked down their meal, they attempted to listen.

One table spoke of leaving Terin for Rayacre. With no prospect for jobs here, they thought they would have a better chance elsewhere. Though they were not sure they would be able to handle the long month's journey to reach it.

The table to their right appeared to be on a date and spoke softly to one another. Their hands embraced across the table, and their eyes never left one another. These two taverns had no information for them.

The third, Monesdep, however, was of more use to them. This tavern was cleaner than the last two had been. The tables and chairs matched each other and did not look as worn. There were not as many patrons to be found in this tavern. They were plenty spaced out, so they had to split up to be able to listen in on all of them.

Fi, Selain, and Alexandria sat near a table with three burly men and a table of two homely-looking women. Iam and Erlan sat near a table of two men speaking in hushed tones. Fi worried slightly about Iam and Erlan being paired together, but they did well from what she could tell.

The two men spoke about leaving Adonia. This brought back memories of the night in Moburn. Jasper and Tobias had been speaking about the same thing before they had turned on her. She would leave Alexandria or Selain to continue listening. Fi did not think her heart could listen to that conversation again. It was the two women who would give her a piece to the puzzle.

"Have you 'eard about that cursed village, Mags?" one of the women asked the other. "You know the one, you get close enough to its borders you feel a cold sensation. I've 'eard it fills your whole body with fear till your feet won't move no more."

"That's an old tale they tell the children to scare them," Mags said back to the other woman. "I swear, Juniper, you are so gullible. Next thing I know, you will be heading straight south trying to find it."

Fi perked up at this conversation. A haunted village that caused feelings of fear. Could this have been caused by magic? They did not have a clue to the depths of the power Fi could wield. It was completely possible this village was protected by magic. Once in the rooms for the night, Fi relayed what she had heard to everyone. They agreed their best course of action was to head south.

"We just have to keep going south," Alexandria said to Selain's whining. "Fi heard there was a village south of Terin that seemed like a good possibility for what we are looking for. We just haven't found it yet."

"All we have been doing is going south. If this is even south at all. This place is so messed up. Finding the position of the sun beneath the clouds is difficult. We could be heading north for all we know!" Selain shot back, clearly fed up with the constant travel.

"Do you have a better idea? If you do, please grace us with it," Iam growled. They were all hot and in a foul mood from traveling in the heat and coming up empty-handed. Selain opened her mouth to answer but closed it as she had no other ideas.

Dinner that night, while better at Erlan's hands, was miserable. Everyone was losing the drive they had when the journey started. A dark cloud loomed, keeping them from finding their goal. They ate in silence and crawled into their bedrolls without another word. Fi hoped they would find the village soon.

As morning came, the clouds had cleared, revealing a scorching day ahead. Beads of sweat formed on Fi's brow, running into her eyes and causing them to burn. How anyone lived in a country like this was beyond her. There was no redeeming quality she could find. Unless there was something she was missing.

Hours into their ride, they spied what looked to be a town in the distance. A rather small town, but it might have a tavern to offer them a reprieve from the day's heat. Or better yet, a real bed to sleep in rather than the hard and dirty ground.

The town was a lot smaller than they anticipated. On the main dirt road they rode in on, they spotted the far edge of town leading back into the desert. To call this a town would be giving it a lot more credit than it offered. There were few buildings erected in what looked like the main part of town. A larger building sat in the center, which appeared to be better cared for. Fi remembered how cared for the temple was in Baydell and wondered if it, too, was a temple.

The further they got into town, the more they noticed there was no life here. No sign of movement from any of the buildings could be found. Not a single child or adult could be seen wandering the streets. It was almost eerie how calm the town was. The wind did not seem to blow as hard through the town.

They found a small stable to secure their horses. There

were no other horses housed when they got there. The town seemed completely abandoned. Their next course of action was to investigate and look for anyone.

"This is kind of spooky," Fi said. "Where is everybody?"

"Maybe they decided to leave and find somewhere closer to a large city," Iam said. Though what he said made sense, there was a feeling Fi could not shake. Something was off about the town being empty. It felt wrong, and she could not describe why.

On a building near the large building they passed, read a sign: Red Worm Tavern. They pushed the door open to find it as empty as the stables. The chairs, however, were not skillfully placed by the table as if the pub were closed. The tables were overturned, and the chairs were broken. Splinters lay across the tavern, and the bar was broken in multiple places.

The perplexing thing was the scorch marks on the walls and floor. A fire had clearly been in those spots, yet there was no way to build a fire where some were. A large angry scorch mark marred the ceiling. There was no logical explanation as to how it could have gotten there except...

Fi looked down at her hand as a tiny ember formed in her hand. No one noticed the marks Fi saw.

Alexandria's hand instantly went to the hilt of her sword. A fight happened in this room and, from the lack of dust, it did not happen long ago. It could have been as recent as before they showed up. There was a strong chance whoever attacked this town was still here, waiting to ambush them.

"Alexandria, the scorch mark by the ceiling I think—" Fi tried to say.

"Shhh. Be quiet," Alexandria snapped back, cutting off mid-sentence. Her eyes darted around the room, looking for any sign of someone being with them. Moving to the bar, Alexandria peered over it, expecting to find an enemy crouched there. She found nothing but empty glasses and bottles of liquor. "Stay here with Fi. I am going to go check the rooms in back."

Without another word, she slipped down a hallway, which Fi assumed were the rooms at the inn. Selain, Erlan, and Iam surrounded Fi from all sides. She was completely protected should someone try to attack her before Alexandria returned.

Time crawled by as they waited for Alexandria to come back. FI's mind feared the worst. Alexandria could have been jumped by who knows how many attackers and overtaken. What if she was lying in pain right now and none of them knew it? It really should not take this long for someone to search such a small tavern. Five minutes later, Alexandria returned with her sword in its scabbard.

"I didn't find anybody, but the rooms have been ransacked. Whoever was here was looking for something," Alexandria said. While her sword was put away, she did not let her guard down. "I do not think we should stay here too much longer."

"Alex—" Fi tried to mention the scorch marks to her again.

"There is too much risk if we stay here. There is no guarantee that whoever did this isn't still here, or if they are coming back." Alexandria ignored Fi yet again.

"ALEXANDRIA!" Fi yelled, having had enough. Everyone turned to her in surprise. "Have you failed to notice the burns near the ceiling? Tell me how a normal person would build a fire so high on a wall without the use of magic?" Everyone turned to look where Fi gestured. All their eyes grew wide, coming to the realization Fi had already come to. They had found the village they were looking for. Only no one was here, wizard or not.

"We will have to brave the danger and continue to look through the village. There has to be some clue about where they went or what has happened here," Erlan said. "This is what we have spent all this time looking for. There has to be answers here somewhere."

"Would it be faster if we split up to look for whatever it is we are looking for?" Selain asked. "You know, divide and conquer."

"Normally, I would agree, but we are in unknown territory with possible enemies hiding nearby. I think it would be best to stick together," said Erlan, and Alexandria nodded, agreeing with him.

They spent the next few hours searching the small buildings in the village. It should not have taken so long, but they wanted to be thorough in case they missed some clue. The homes were simple, many just having a bed and table. It reminded Fi of the dwelling they occupied in Pirn. Everything had a purpose, and nothing without one was kept.

Though there were no signs of people, there was no dust left on the furniture. Whatever had happened must have happened recently. As in the tavern, the furniture was upturned, and the mattresses sliced open. What could they have been looking for?

Once finished with the dwellings, they moved on to the large building in the middle of the village. As they drew closer, Fi felt a hum in her ears. It reminded her of cicadas in the night. She looked around to see if anyone else reacted. Yet no one's expression changed. With every step towards the building, the humming intensified. It was not loud enough to impede her hearing but enough to be bothersome.

As Fi thought, it appeared to be a temple of some kind. Though it was not tended to in a way to give the goddess justice. It housed no windows but a set of doors. The large, heavy double door creaked open as both Erlan and Iam pushed on them. Inside was dimly lit and hard to see. However, on the far side of the room, a large mound of something was visible.

They slowly made their way forward, unsure what it was they were to find. Everyone took a step back as the mound turned out to be a pile of bodies they assumed were the villagers. A feeling pulled Fi forward, and she went to examine the corpses. Iam went to grab her arm, but she shook him off. She had to look closer.

Their faces were sunk in and shriveled. Hollowed eyes stared back at her, pulling her even closer. The humming now peaked in volume. There was nothing left of them but skin and bones. It appeared their very essence had been drained. It was then that something caught Fi's eye. On the arm of the closest body was a similar marking, one she had grown accustomed to.

A delicate line flowed downward while another line crossed the first and curled on the ends. It was the same mark she bore on her shoulder blade. These were marked people, as she was. There truly was a village hidden away until recently.

A hand jutted out then and grabbed her wrist. Fi tried to pull back, but it held firm.

"Leave! Leave before he comes back," the withered man's voice said weakly. Before Fi could answer, everyone was at her side.

"Who? Who could come back? What happened here?" Fi's heart broke seeing them discarded in the way they were. Her body broke out in a cold sweat, fearing who could have done this.

"The one they call Syler. He will surely kill you, too. You are marked as we are, and he will take what he thinks is his." His voice feebly said. Fi's stomach felt as heavy as lead, knowing how close they were to Syler. Did he know she was coming here? Was another misfortune her fault?

"How do you know I am marked?" Fi asked. She quickly glanced at her shoulder, but the mark was still hidden.

"Do you not hear the hum of the magic left here?" His voice rasped. "It is how he found us I am sure of it." It made sense now why she could hear the sound and no one else. She was tapping into the wizard's magic. If Syler could hear it, too, she would have to be even more careful. There would be no hiding in plain sight.

"Let me help you please," Fi said, trying to take off her pack with one hand. She wanted to retrieve her waterskin and try to save the man's life.

"My life is naught. There is no way to save me from what is done. But I must pass on the knowledge before I die." His voice grew quieter as he spoke.

"What are you talking about?" Fi asked. This man made no sense. He refused aid but wanted to give her advice. "Please, let me help you." Fi disregarded his wish and pulled the waterskin from her pack and opened it. She placed the waterskin against his lips, and he took a few gulps before coughing.

"I was told long ago should anything happen to me, this needed to be passed to another who is marked. It needs to stay remembered so it may reach the one we have been waiting for,". he said. "Please, listen. I was given the news of a prophecy the elves possessed." Before he could continue, he broke into another long coughing fit.

"My father already told us the prophecy. In a time of peace, a bringer of turmoil will arise. They will have the power to turn friends against friends and families against themselves. Those once filled with light will be overcome by darkness. Chaos will come before a false sense of peace rests across the land. To stop their infectious spread, the light must be returned. The bringer of light will be marked by matriarchal loss. Save your strength," Erlan said. His eyes were slightly glossed as he looked down at the man before him. His mouth twitched as he finished speaking.

"Indeed, your father knew most of the prophecy I see, but he must have forgotten there was more. In my opinion, it is the most important part. There is another mentioned in the prophecy. What your father forgot was—" The man coughed again before regaining his breath. *"Hidden in the deepest of Abaddon's belly can it be found. Only the one descendant of those who sealed the magic away can release the light and complete those who are marked. It is then that one who can master both will defeat the evil who bestowed the world in darkness."*

Everyone looked at each other, and then at Erlan and Selain. One of them could be the one to truly release the light from the Rune of Calwa. While it did not change their quest, it changed who needed to be protected. Fi turned back to ask the man a question about the one who could harness both, but he laid as still as stone against the ground. She slipped her hand from his and said a prayer to the goddess.

"What do you think it all means?" Iam asked, looking as shocked as everyone else.

"It's obvious, isn't it?" Fi said, almost feeling a weight off her shoulders. The pressure of being the prophesied one was lifted. "Either Erlan or Selain needs to release the magic of Calwa, but until we find it, we won't know which it is. So, our next step will be to find the rune."

"Okay, but we don't even know where to look. We are back at square one with nowhere to go," Selain said. She roughly ran her fingers through her short, golden blonde hair.

"Yes, we do. He said the deepest depth of Abaddon. If you had to go deep into the ground, where would you go?" asked Alexandria. Everyone looked at each other, feeling they were missing an obvious answer right in front of them. "Kaweil, the land of the dwarves. No one digs further into the ground than their mines go."

"That's brilliant," Fi said. "Okay. Let's make our way to see the dwarves. We should leave here as soon as possible because, as he said, we don't know if Syler is coming back." Even saying his name ran a shiver up Fi's spine. The evil this man possessed was unfathomable.

They quickly made their way back to the horses. Fi wanted to stay and properly bury the dead, but they could not stay any longer where they were. She mounted Hero, and using the reins, led him in line with everyone else. She looked back at the village she had set to be her new home. With a new direction, she led Hero away from her fallen wizards. The dwarves now held the hope of Abaddon.

Epilouge

Syler returned to Highbarrow feeling a great amount of satisfaction. He had heard a rumor about a village of hiding wizards but could never prove it existed. In all honesty, it was a completely random chance he had even found it. If he had not been visiting Rayacre and the winds had not been blowing just as they were, he would have never stumbled across it. It was the perfect situation.

The winds caused him to take a different course than he intended. Though it turned out to be just what he needed. The familiar humming found his ears and drew him closer. With the volume the humming came, he knew there had to be more than one. He did not expect a village of nearly twenty rogue wizards.

While the villagers there possessed the mark, they did not know how to use their powers efficiently. Something he had learned and practiced often to master. They used what little they could to keep those who came near the village out. A simple fear spell would cause terror in anyone who came close enough. It really was a brilliant idea. If he needed to use a type of barrier for Highbarrow in the future, he may steal their idea.

However, if anyone were to break through their fear spell,

they were inept in their defense. Not a single adult could conjure a decent elemental spell. Something he was able to easily master soon after touching the rune that bestowed the magic upon him. Only a few could produce even a flame. And those that did had no control over what they did with it. They had no chance of hitting him if they wanted to. What a miserable life it was not to control one's magic. Even worse not to possess it at all. He was grateful he found the rune that changed his life.

He reminisced briefly on the day his life had changed. Before finding the rune, he was a simple knight bent on becoming a paladin in Soeric. He wanted nothing more than to have the power, as he had none. Born to a farmer, he was nobody. Unlike his father, he was not content with only dealing in what life dealt him. He knew if he were to make his mark, he would have to take matters into his own hands.

He worked hard to earn the title of knight. Though everyone knew if you were to be somebody, you needed to be a paladin. They were the trusted guardians of Soeric. That was where the true power lay. High Knights, however, thought him rash and short-tempered. None of these traits would make a good knight let alone a paladin. Syler was told to leave and find another profession.

Angered by their decision he was bent on finding a way to prove them wrong. He traveled to a remote part of Zireven. There were rumors of something rare that could give one the strength to best even the paladins of Soeric. He had underestimated the terrain and the mountains he needed to pass through. His body was ready to give up before he was able to finish his quest.

Syler took refuge in a cave as a snowstorm started in on him.

His hands were numb as he crawled through the rough stone opening. Relief settled over him as he was no longer being assaulted by the winds of the storm. It did not change the coldness that was still all around him. He was ready to give up hope of surviving the foolhardy trip.

It was then he came across it, Nulla, the rune of darkness. Though he did not know what it was at the time, he had found it. Syler felt a pull to the dark jagged looking stone that lay in the mountainside. Tucked in a cave, it was long forgotten by whomever it was that had left it there. Compulsion raged over him to touch it and as he laid a hand upon it, he felt a sensation rock through him unlike anything he had felt before. A burst of force surged forward, throwing him up against the cave wall. When he awoke, he was a changed man, never to be the same.

It was hard to believe over five hundred years had passed since the day he released magic back upon the world. Not intentionally, of course. He would have rather not shared this power with anyone. Those born with the mark, such as his, did have their uses, however. He was walking the halls of Highbarrow when he was pulled from his thoughts.

"Welcome home, my love," said an auburn-haired woman. Her hazel eyes were warm as she looked upon her husband. "Highbarrow never feels the same without you here. Did you succeed in the task you set out to complete?"

His raven, Stolas, was perched upon her shoulder. Upon seeing him, he flew over and landed on Syler's shoulder. Stolas preened his feathers now back upon his master. It was not often Syler was without him. Though on formal diplomatic trips, it was best he stayed in Highbarrow. He found he seemed to put the monarchs at unease.

"I did. And on the way back I found so much more. Soon I will have enough to not only have the trust of everyone in Abaddon but to take it from them and rule in their stead." He placed his muscled arm around his wife and walked with her deeper into Highbarrow. A deep purple amulet glowed brightly against his chest.

Made in the USA
Middletown, DE
15 April 2022